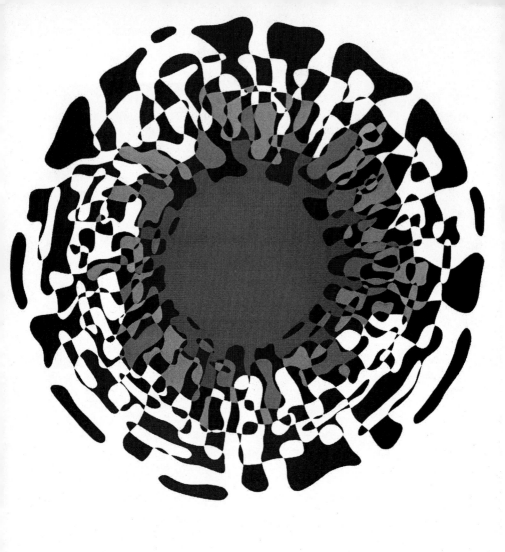

Donald Breckenridge

Starcherone Books Buffalo, NY

YOU ARE HERE

Cover Illustration: Bruce Pearson
Editor: Ted Pelton
Cover and Book Design: Rebecca Maslen
Proofreading: Christine Webb

First Edition

Library of Congress Cataloging-in-Publication Data
Breckenridge, Donald.
  You are here / Donald Breckenridge.
     p. cm.
  ISBN 978-0-9788811-8-4 (alk. paper)
  1. City and town life--New York (State)--New York--Fiction.
  2. New York (N.Y.)--Fiction. I. Title.
  PS3552.R3619Y68 2009
  813'.54--dc22
                              2008044916

YOU ARE HERE

for Johannah Rodgers

Beauty is a precarious trace that eternity causes to appear to us and that it takes away from us. A manifestation of eternity, and a sign of death as well. Often it seems to me to be an evil flower of nothingness, or else the cry of the world as it dies, or a desperate, sumptuous prayer.

And then ashes.

The light has blinded me. But it has stopped me. Otherwise I would not be here writing, and suffering from wanting to remember this event which in any case can never be forgotten.

Eugene Ionesco (Present Past, Past Present)

Mid-April and late October

The light from my desk lamp fell upon the conversation between Janet, "Oh, it's for my benefit," a childless divorcee in her mid-forties who was living off a substantial monthly stipend from her second husband. And James, "Do you think," a twenty-four year old aspiring writer who worked part-time in a used bookstore, "I should write that down?" They were seated on a recently repainted bench in Union Square. She opened her purse, "here's my pen," and handed it to him. It was a warm Thursday afternoon in mid-October, approximately five miles and six months away from the desk where I was fleshing out their conversation. He took the pointed cap off the ballpoint pen, "I'll put it right here," and placed the tip to his open palm. Most of the leaves on the trees in the park had already turned brown. "Use it sparingly," she had a warm smile, "like a good cologne—" "I got that part," he looked at her from above the rims of his glasses, "Now, what about your phone number?" She was almost afraid that he wasn't going to ask, "What could you possibly want with that?" "Because I'd like to see you again," he stole another glance at her knees encased in shimmering gray stockings while venturing, "unless of course—" "Oh no," she shook her head, "this has been so much fun I'd love to see you again." They'd met at The Strand three hours ago, "Yeah it has," then moved to a quiet booth in the rear of a nearby Greek diner, "it's been a great day," where their conversation expanded over cups of watery coffee, day-old chocolate éclairs and tepid chamomile tea. This park bench allowed for a last brief exchange. James smiled, "I'm really glad that I came into the city." When she laughed in the sunlight he noticed that most of her teeth were capped. "Why is that so funny?" Shaking her head, "you sound so provincial when you say that," before discovering an orange smudge on the right front pocket of her beige raincoat. "I like Brooklyn," he muttered. "Your neighborhood is quite beautiful but…" Janet scraped at the smudge with her unpainted thumbnail and then wet her forefinger with the tip of her tongue, "I have some friends who live near you," before rubbing it into the faint smudge. He grinned, "Are they yuppies or writers?" She examined the damp spot on her pocket, "neither …" and finally satisfied she replied, "they're lesbians." A police helicopter flew overhead and the sound reverberated off the buildings surrounding the park. "Why am I not surprised?" The sleeves of his dark grey shirt were frayed at the cuffs and the collar was worn down along the crease. Locks of her magenta hair were rearranged by the breeze as she said, "I'll have to tell them to keep an eye on you." He held up his hands in surrender, "I'm in real trouble now." She turned to him and quietly asked, "Do I look like trouble to you?" He studied her dark brown eyes, "not at all," and sensual pout, "but I guess it's only fair for me to ask you the same question." She kissed him just above the faint stubble on his cheek, "I'll give you my number but you have to use it," leaving a soft impression with her auburn lipstick. "Of course," he began to blush as she whispered it in his ear. He wrote the ten digits on the palm of his left hand then recapped the pen, "thank you," and handed it back. She placed the pen in her purse, "you're quite welcome," snapped the clasp, "and now if you don't mind I'd like to walk you to your train." He leaned back, "So soon?" She stood up, "I'm afraid so," and smoothed down her skirt. He placed his hands on his knees, "but we were just getting started." "We've got to save a few discoveries," she glanced at the thin platinum watch on her left wrist, "for the next time." James swayed a bit as he stood up. She slid her hands into the pockets of her raincoat while walking next to him, "Will you call me?" The coffee was percolating on the stove. "Of course." They stopped before a flight of stairs that lead to the turnstiles. I yawned while stretching my arms above my head. James watched a few people descending the stairs before turning to her and saying, "I guess this is my stop."

I stood up and yawned again while walking to the kitchen and then used a green dishtowel to hold the pot while pouring coffee into my white cup. Yesterday, Carly Simon was singing about the clouds in her coffee while I was buying spinach and tomatoes for dinner at the Korean market on 7th avenue. A dollop of milk turned my coffee dark brown. As I sat at the desk a blond woman wearing an orange T-shirt, dark blue shorts and white sneakers jogged by. "Can we see each other next week?" His question brightened the grin on her face. An ambulance sped through the nearby intersection. She nodded, "I know a good place for coffee and it isn't very expensive." The chorus of sparrows continued chirping outside the open window on my left as the siren faded down the avenue. "Okay," she kissed him quickly on both cheeks, "so I'll see you next week." He smiled and then walked down the flight of stairs. She waved dutifully when he looked back, then turned and walked toward the corner.

13

Four National Guardsmen cradling machine guns were milling around the token booth. A bike messenger was nearly hit by a taxi making a U-turn in the intersection. James removed the MetroCard from his wallet as the man in front of him re-swiped his card. The splayed remains of a pigeon were crumpled in the gutter beneath Janet. The prerecorded message from the MTA urging customers to report any suspicious packages or activities was broadcasted as he pushed through the turnstile and walked through the station. The pedestrians entering the crosswalk moved quickly toward the opposite sides of the street. A Brooklyn-bound Q train was pulling up to the platform as he descended the stairs. She weighed their prospects for happiness while stepping over the curb and allowed herself a narrow smile. "The next stop will be Canal Street," James entered the crowded train and looked for a seat, "step all the way in and stand clear of the closing doors." The drugstore windows she walked by were decorated with ghosts, goblins, and large spiders that dangled from imitation webs. He gripped the metal pole with his right hand as the train lurched out of the station. A portion of the sun hung below a bank of orange clouds. He studied the smudged, but still legible, blue numbers on his palm. She removed a pair of mirrored sunglasses from her purse and put them on. He swayed into the shoulder of the person beside him as the train rounded the curve before speeding past the 8th Street station. A slow moving plane was silhouetted by the setting sun. He thought about how pretty she looked while sitting across from him at the diner. Janet glanced at her reflection as it was cast on a row of tinted windows. James remarked, "they make a really good cheeseburger here," as she looked over the menu in silent bemusement. Long shadows on the sidewalk were stretched beneath the pedestrians. Shaking her head, "go ahead if you're hungry," while closing the menu, "I've already had lunch." She removed her sunglasses before entering the pet store. He shrugged, "I'm okay," having eaten a large breakfast around noon, "maybe I'll just get a pastry." She headed down the narrow aisle toward a row of shelves displaying cat toys. "So when you're not working in a used bookstore you're hanging out in one?" The yellow price tag dangled from the ear of a large blue and green cloth mouse. "Pretty much," he grinned, "and you?" She walked to the counter and placed the toy before the man seated behind the cash register. "I was just running an errand and thought that I might find something new to read," then coyly added, "while cruising for boys." The man counted out her change before putting the mouse in a small white plastic bag. "Oh," his eyes widened, "do you live nearby?" She began walking home. "Not too far." He gripped the metal pole with both hands as the train reached Canal Street. "And when you're not hanging out in used bookstores you're writing fiction?" He leaned into the young woman reading a paperback as the train came to a slow screeching stop. "Yeah, it's kind of sick when you think about it." She shook her head, "I don't think so." The doors opened at Canal Street. He looked down at the table and smiled, "No?" "Step all the way into the car," a crowd of elderly Chinese women carrying light red plastic shopping bags boarded the train, "and stand clear of the closing doors." "I think it shows your level of commitment." The woman with the paperback was able to squeeze between two potbellied MTA workers wearing battered hardhats and steel-toed boots. "I really don't have much of a life." The doors closed and quickly reopened, "we're being held in the station by supervision dispatch," as three police officers, "and should be proceeding shortly," with bulletproof vests bulging beneath their uniforms, "thank you for your patience," made their way into the packed car. "What do you like to do for fun?" He shook his head, "not much," and placidly stated, "go to parties or bars," then scratched his chin, "a friend of mine lives out on Far Rockaway with his girlfriend and sometimes I spend the weekends with them." On the first Sunday in September the three of them had sat on the beach a few hours before dawn and smoked a joint as an infrequent procession of planes flew out of JFK. "The next stop on this Brooklyn-bound Q train will be DeKalb Avenue." The three police officers talked about batting averages while standing around the metal pole. The amphora on the cover of the menu was smeared with orange frosting. A long row of bright lights lining the walls of the tunnel passed by the vibrating windows. She noted his torn cuticles while scrutinizing the size of his hands. Sunlight flooded the packed compartment as the train began crossing the Manhattan Bridge. He took the dark red plastic cup filled with ice water off the table.

An Older Lover —Act 1

Three stage lights went up in a slow twenty count as the scattered conversations around me concluded. The man and woman seated on the beige folding metal chairs were facing each other. He was wearing a dark green suit, "I think we'd be able to tell the difference," glasses with thin black frames and black leather shoes. She was wearing a sleeveless low-cut short black dress, "How so?" fishnets and black patent leather pumps with three-inch heels. A couple that happened to be seated in the audience were being portrayed onstage. They just had dinner in a dimly lit West Village restaurant that had recently been awarded two stars in the *Times* and praise for its romantic ambience, esoteric wine list and above average French food. "It's in their body language," he was halfway through his third glass of Crozes-Hermitage, "now don't turn around." The woman discreetly turned and studied the young fashionable couple tucked into an oversized booth across the dining room. "It isn't *that* obvious." Cindy had found most of the actor's costume on the racks and in the bins of the Salvation Army on Flatbush Avenue last week. His short brown hair had been set with styling gel, "I didn't say that it was obvious." The rings on her left hand caught the stage lights as she accompanied her question with a gesture, "Are you sure that you're not projecting your own insecurities?" "Please," he furrowed his brow, "they're trying too hard." The actress who was portraying the wealthy, childless divorcee in her mid forties, "You really like watching people," had purchased her dress online and wore it during almost every rehearsal. Her thick hair was cropped into a bob and had recently been dyed magenta. He'd been too distracted by their conversation, "they are like a Diane Arbus photograph," to do more than half-heartedly pick at the herb encrusted roast chicken she suggested he order for his entrée. Her cheeks had been heavily powdered and the dark red lipstick carefully painted on and around her lips gave her face a corpse-like pallor. He then added, "without chemistry." She had been instructed to carry herself with warm outspoken urgency, "my husband was like that," to compensate for their difference in age, "when we—" He nervously blurted, "Like what?" "Just like you silly," she cleared her throat, "he really enjoys watching people." He shifted in the metal chair, "I guess it's not all that uncommon," that creaked beneath him. The wine and the warmth of their repartee had almost invalidated the cloying embarrassment he felt whenever the tall gay waiter hovered over their table with his incessant questions about the food: if it was seasoned to their liking, how well the wine he recommended paired with their entrees and, most recently, while taking their plates away, if they had given any thought to dessert. "Do you know her work?" Tilting her head to the left, "Who?" He regarded her expression before saying, "Diane Arbus." "Of course," she has a quick wit and a half dozen credit cards nestled in her calfskin wallet, "I'd love to own one of her photographs." He imagined the art on the walls of her apartment in a nearby prewar building. A black and white Warhol silkscreen hung above the couch in the living room where a longhaired chocolate colored cat just woke from her evening nap. A framed poster from G.W. Pabst's, *Diary of a Lost Girl* hung on the wall above the Mackintosh table and chairs in the dining room. He commented on the framed, autographed poster from a Kiki Smith retrospective on the kitchen wall opposite the sink as she mixed their drinks. She handed him a scotch and water with a wink while asking if he'd like to see the etchings on the ceiling in her bedroom. Cindy was biting her lower lip in frustration while scribbling... *Diane Arbus... where is your focus????* in her wire-bound notebook. The actress turned to observe the couple in the audience before claiming, "he is nothing more than the latest way for her to wear her hair." Cindy wanted to know, and wanted the audience to be clearly aware of what her character's emotional investments were. He smiled, "And for him?" Cindy repeatedly insisted that although they were portraying nameless caricatures they had to remain in the moment at all times. "And for him..." after another careful look over her shoulder she stated, "she is nothing more than a new pair of shoes," in a cool matter of fact tone. Over the coming weeks she will reach the conclusion that their relationship must have constituted an interesting life experience for him and will occasionally wonder how he will portray her in his fiction. "Are you sure that you're not projecting your own insecurities?" She swallowed hard, "sweetheart," while searching his face, "I didn't mean anything by that." He noticed how the crows-feet etched around her dark brown eyes were starting to show through her makeup. "Then why did you ask me that?" Knowing if she strays too far from the persona he began fashioning for her long before they actually met, "you're being so sensitive," that this date and any subsequent encounters will be total disasters. He shrugged, "Aren't women into that?" "Oh it's for my benefit," she is incapable of being alone and afraid of being hurt in another relationship, "well that is very flattering."

There were many days when she was unable to get out of bed and subsisted on whole-wheat crackers, warm mineral water, the fickle affection of her cat, Esther, and sleep as the afternoons dragged into late mornings while the shifting blue glow from her bedroom television covered her pale face and bare limbs like a warm muted blanket. He will later insist that this relationship was simply an exploration of the roles and preconceived notions of romantic love. The unlikely vow they took later that night, upon her faintly perfumed sheets, was to love one another with as few inhibitions as possible and without any emotional strings attached until the end of the year.

While placing her elbows on the table, "Don't you want to know what she is thinking right now?" "Sure," he shrugged, "why not?" "Well she is hoping that everyone here will notice how beautiful she looks in that new dress," before glancing over her shoulder, "although she is a bit disappointed that there aren't that many people here yet… which is odd especially considering that *Times* review," then rested her chin in the narrow palm of her left hand, "but maybe if they linger over dessert she'll get a larger audience." "Oh really," he squeezed his knees, "and how do you know that?" During their first date last Thursday afternoon in the rear of a dimly lit Tribeca café, he had carefully floated the idea of his experiment past her. "She is a real type." It happened after the first awkward pause in their conversation, after they had exhausted an extensive list of writers that he admired. He stole another glance at the couple across the restaurant as the skepticism in his voice, "I guess," betrayed him. It was just after she had finished her second cup of chamomile tea. She shifted in the metal chair, "I was once very close to a woman like that." As the opening strains of Bruckner's 6th were piped in through the café speakers, he politely asked her if he could talk about himself. "Do you think you still have anything in common with the woman sitting across from us?" She batted her eyelashes while confessing that she found him fascinating and assured him that nothing would be more interesting than learning more about him.

What followed was a carefully prepared and well-rehearsed twenty-minute monologue that began with a detailed description of his unhappy childhood and concluded with his proposal concerning romantic love.

He was an only child of divorced parents, he had endured a stifling upper middle-class suburban upbringing and attended a private liberal arts college in the northeast that was well known for its creative writing program. She was informed that his professional prospects were quite good and that although he was so young a few of his stories had already been published in quarterly journals and monthly magazines and achieved, to a certain degree, critical acclaim. He had recently made the acquaintance of the assistant to a highly sought after agent and believed that it was only a matter of time before his first collection of short stories would be picked up by a major publishing house for a hefty sum. He then speculated that, even though the major houses weren't publishing many short story collections from young writers, with the help of his soon to be agent and a handful of well placed and carefully tended relationships with powerful editors it could easily turn out to be a bestseller. With watery blue eyes widening behind fashionable frames, he wistfully described the power he would soon be wielding in the publishing industry. Claiming that he had everything he wanted, everything he hoped for in his young life had been attained and yet he had never experienced love. She stopped herself from remarking *that so few of us, especially people like us, ever do experience love* and simply nodded before gazing thoughtfully at the urine colored dregs in the bottom of her tea cup. He appraised her silent response before confidently adding that he was certain that with her—and only with her—a woman twice his age—could he truly come to understand just what it meant to be in love. This was because she had known love, as any woman as beautiful must have on countless occasions, and because, and here he paused long enough to prepare the delivery, she had thus far lived a full, and by her own acknowledgment, an interesting life. She was silently flattered by all of his false assumptions.

"It was just neglect that ended our relationship," both hands were now cradling her chin, "and the less time we spent together," as she sighed, "the more I realized how little we had in common." He leaned back in the chair while asking, "And how long ago was this?" A slight smile creased her lips, "when everyone I knew had a ton of money and when you were just starting high school." He wiped his palms on his knees before delivering the next question, "And how did you become friends in the first place?" She folded her pale hands on the table, "we were never really friends," and tilted her head to the left, "we were lovers." "I didn't know that you were—" "I'm not really," a blush dimmed her powdered cheeks, "it was just a phase." "Like the way you wore your hair?" "Exactly," she smiled through his last line then quickly added, "the skirts that spring were very short." The following Wednesday afternoon she called him at the bookstore because she had somehow managed to get early dinner reservations at that new French restaurant in Chelsea on the same day it was reviewed in the *Times*. He swallowed hard before placing both feet on the stage, "What was it like?" And then he briefly described a two-act play being performed that night on the Lower East Side and asked if she wanted to do that after dinner. "I prefer men." She said it sounded more interesting than that movie she'd been reading so much about before brightly suggesting that they should go back to her place for a nightcap afterwards. Clearing his throat, "Physically?" He clutched the telephone receiver with both hands while being told that she simply loved the short story he gave her last Thursday, and then added that it was well written. "Physically I guess, but we can talk more about that later." He leaned forward, "How many women were you with?" She asked, "Encounters or relationships?" and before he could respond she confessed, "I was either very lonely or deeply cynical." He placed his elbows on the table, "Why, can't it be both?" They had met at The Strand three weeks ago. "I suppose it would depend on what day of the week you asked me." They were standing on opposite ends of a display table when he caught her eye. "Isn't that how you described your second marriage?" She had been thumbing through a remaindered copy of *The Satyricon* before acknowledging his attention with a discreet nod. "Now be very careful you…" while waving a narrow index finger in front of his face, "young man."

Portrait of a Girl 4/20/04

Jonny was awakened at seven-thirty by the travel alarm clock on the nightstand. After feeding the cats he prepared a large pot of coffee. The kitchen window overlooked an iron fire escape that ended a storey above the cement courtyard where a mourning dove was nested on the branch of a dead tree. The radio on the kitchen counter: a car commercial, stock quotes and then the weather, mostly sunny and a bit cooler than yesterday with an afternoon high around seventy-six and a low tonight around fifty-seven, followed by continuing coverage of the Marines' bloody siege in Fallujah and more on the story of that near fatal Long Island Railroad crash at Penn Station yesterday morning that injured one hundred and twenty-seven people. Jonny removed his pajamas in the bathroom and took a long, hot shower. His wife turned over in her sleep as he combed his hair with damp fingers in the mirror above the mahogany dresser. Jonny sat at the kitchen table drinking a large cup of coffee. The paperback on the table, Kenneth Chambers' illustrated biography of Bela Bartok, was opened to the chapter entitled "Portrait of a Girl 1907-'09." The black and white photograph of almost a dozen peasants standing alongside a farmhouse as the young composer prepared a wax cylinder—*Bartok recording folk-song in 1907, in Darza, Nyitra County, now Drazovce, Slovakia.* He stirred a spoonful of sugar into the cup of coffee for his wife and carried it into their bedroom before kissing her goodbye. He took the book off the table and slipped it into his black canvas shoulder bag. The front door locked behind him as it closed. A bulging, semi-transparent shopping bag smelling of bacon grease was knotted up outside the neighbor's door. A diffused block of sunlight covered a portion of the dark blue-green and gray floor tiles as he walked down the hall. The long fluorescent bulbs encased in frosted plastic frames were humming along the center of the ceiling as the elevator appeared behind the shatterproof window. Jonny pulled open the outer green door as the inner steel door slid sideways to reveal the imitation wood-panel interior.

I had called him the night before to see if he would be interested in designing the sound for a two-act play that I had hoped to stage in the fall. He told me that he would be happy to and then wanted to know what the play was about. "The first act is a half-hour long conversation between a young man and an older woman who are on a date in a West Village restaurant, and the second act takes place on a bench in Bowling Green Park and that's another conversation, this time between a married man and the young woman he's having an affair with."

Jonny slowly descended a flight of stairs at the subway entrance while removing the MetroCard from his wallet. He entered the car behind two elderly women and sat down as the doors closed. The man seated across from him unfolded his copy of the *Times* as the Manhattan bound N train pulled out of the station. The color photograph on the front page featured two rebels brandishing AK-47's while standing in front of a burning Humvee.

The bartender flicked through the static filled channels on the muted television with the remote in his right hand. Cindy stood up and walked toward the doors as the Q train slowed before the Atlantic Avenue station. The condensation from the brown beer bottle had created a circular watermark on the coaster. The male passengers looked at her as she inspected her reflection in the window— wearing a knee-length black dress, black ankle socks and black shoes with thick heels.

Andrew had watched the occasional headlights streak across the bedroom ceiling while recalling Cindy's soundless sleep during the two years they had shared his bed. The female conductor listed the available transfers, "to the D, 2, 3, 4, 5, and the Long Island Railroad," as the train came to a screeching stop, "please take all of your personal belongings with you and have a safe and pleasant day." A reproduction of the red white and blue label on the beer bottle was printed on the damp coaster. She stepped out of the car and walked toward the exit indicated by the red arrow spray-painted on the wall. The bourbon in the highball glass was a shade lighter than the bar beneath it. Her steps were punctuated by the sound of sledgehammers demolishing a wall as she climbed a flight of stairs. Andrew wanted to nestle into Cindy's side and let the warm smell of her skin calm him to sleep. The broad intersection and low-lying buildings appeared before her. He fell asleep at dawn and had a series of violent, inconclusive dreams before waking up just in time to call in sick. The advertisement on the side of the bus stop for a new antidepressant featured an attractive brunette in her early thirties standing in the center of an elegantly furnished living room, dressed in a beige business suit and speaking on a cordless phone. The long mirror framed Andrew sitting alone in the empty bar. Swollen white clouds hung in the hazy blue sky as her black hair was blown off her shoulders by an afternoon breeze. A program devoted to the music Lester Young recorded with The Oscar Peterson Trio was playing quietly on the radio. Cindy's cell phone began to vibrate in her purse as she crossed the congested intersection. The hands on the Budweiser clock above the bar mirror indicated that it was five minutes till one.

An automated voice instructed me to leave a message after the tone. "Hey Cindy it's Donald, I called your apartment last night and Andrew gave me this number. I guess you've moved… anyway I was wondering if you would be interested in taking a look at … and maybe directing this play I'm working on… I've just about finished it and I think you'll like it… Also I think I might have a space to mount it in the fall. So give me a call sometime if you're interested."

Andrew listened to Cindy's heels on the barroom tiles as she walked toward him.

An Older Lover – Act 1

"You just don't," he backpedaled, "I mean… you just don't seem like that sort of person," while searching the candlelit table between them for something to add, "I guess that—" "And what sort of person is that?" "You know," he clenched his fists, "the sort of person who would just collect experiences for the sake of," and allowed his voice to trail off into the multiple conversations surrounding them, "the experience." She leaned forward to be heard over the restaurant noise, "but that's exactly what you're doing." He crossed his arms over his stomach and frowned. "Well," she was relieved by his sullen response, "perhaps I've misunderstood you." He stared at the table in silence. She gently suggested, "but we might not have had that in common." He glanced at her face before asking, "No?" She needed to dispel her suspicions about his underlying motives, "no absolutely not," while acknowledging her insecurities, "all of the things that were important to me then seem so superficial now," and added, "although all of those encounters became relationships," while regarding the lipstick traces along the rim of her nearly empty wine glass. "Would you like to go somewhere else after dinner… instead of that play?" "No," shaking her head, "why do you ask?" He shrugged his shoulders and sighed. "Please don't mope," she placed her left hand on top his right, "I find that so unappealing." He examined the rings on her fingers, "all of my questions," while wondering if they were gifts from former lovers, "some people think that I'm very intrusive." She reached across the table, "no sweetheart," and caressed his chin, "Besides how else will we get to know each other?" He gazed at the reassuring look in her eyes, "I just don't want you to think I'm using you." "I don't," holding up her left hand, "and I'm not," as if taking an oath, "and I'll never," while shaking her head from side to side, "I swear." The clatter of dishes punctuated the pause between them as she noticed a portion of the dimly lit dining room behind her faintly reflected in the corners of his glasses.

Labor Day and Cold Spring

Janet was on the couch, "please don't shout at me," with her pale legs tucked beneath her. Mark was seated across from her, "I'm not angry with you," in the leather-bound chair to the right of the open window. Janet shook her head, "then don't raise your voice," and watched his expression cloud with disdain. Mark already sounded, "just what did you expect," worn out by the explanation he assumed she would now demand. As Janet stood, "let me freshen your drink," she wondered where Esther had run off to. Mark held out his glass, "please."

Her pale bare feet crossed the parquet floor as the car alarm a few blocks away began again. She checked her lipstick in the small oval mirror above the kitchen sink before filling their tall green glasses with Gilbey's, a few cubes of ice from the freezer and a splash of tonic.

Mark placed his cell phone on the side table. Janet handed him the drink and asked, "How can you be such a bad liar?" With a shrug, "I didn't think you'd care." She sat on the couch, "I don't," and crossed her right leg over her left knee. He was alternately regarding the drink in his hand, "then why bring it up," and her bare thighs. She slowly kicked her leg back and forth, "Is she very beautiful?" The gin gradually numbed his tongue, "yes," as he sipped the drink. They had been seeing each other casually, "I'm sure she is," since mid-April, "and how," and Janet had endured four months of his adamant insistence that their relationship shouldn't become too serious, "And how did you meet?" The suspicions that had plagued her were now grounded in all of his artless excuses. "Through a friend." She bit her lower lip, "Anyone I know?" Mark was convinced that this would be their last encounter, "perhaps," at least for a few months. "And how

long ago was this?" "Last year," he cleared his throat, "last summer...."
before meeting her expectant look for the first time since she returned
from the kitchen, "we're getting married in October." Her foot came to
a slow stop next to her ankle, "everyone is doing that now..." he raised
his eyebrows and that prompted her to elaborate, "autumn weddings,"
then ask, "Where?" Mark weighed his response, "East Hampton...
at her parent's new place," before taking another sip, "Did you put
enough gin in this?" She shrugged, "And that's where she is now?"
He suppressed a smile, "until Monday night." "Does she care?" He
shook his deeply tanned shaved head, "she doesn't know." "So she
would if she did?" "Precisely." Janet took a measured sip, "her first,"
then brushed the spray of bubbles off the tip of her nose. He waited
before asking, "First what?" She looked up from yesterday's pedicure,
"marriage." A nod. The weary grin that pulled at the corners of her
painted mouth, "so that's why you..." revealed the drawn currents
beneath her makeup, "didn't bring me any flowers." His smile, "I
should have brought some limes," exhibited both rows of polished
teeth, "you know I'll miss you." She leaned forward and placed her
drink on the floor before looking up, "you are such," and noticed that
he was fixated on her breasts, "an idiot." He gripped the armrests and
stood, "shall we go to bed," with a look of relief.

The fond memories from Janet's second marriage, "I needed a
change of scenery," were propagated by being in Cold Spring, "and
wanted to go to Dia again," and conflicted with the relationship she
was fleeing, "Have you been?" Mark was of average intelligence,
"in Beacon..." dishonest and manipulative, "no I haven't," and often
believed his own lies, "I hear it's very impressive." Janet had been
lilting from panic and unease, "I thought I'd do that tomorrow," to

disbelief and euphoria, "before going home," since arriving by train in the early afternoon. "Why aren't you staying in Beacon?" She awoke alone from her nap in a tastefully furnished bedroom, "I like it here," overlooking a broad expanse of the Hudson around five o'clock, "and besides it's only a cab ride away," as the amber sunlight flooded the windows opposite the broad sleigh bed and fell upon the Turkish carpet covering a portion of the pale oak floor, "then I'll take the train back from there tomorrow," and simply assumed her surroundings were a lingering extension of the dream she hadn't quite woken from. "Where are you staying?" The relief in discovering a distraction, "at a bed and breakfast," seemingly far from home, "down the street," gave confidence to her germinating resolve. Mark was wearing a navy blue blazer, a white dress shirt with an open collar, "Which one," pressed khakis and polished loafers that were resting on the wide brass railing rounding the bottom of the bar, "The Hudson House?" She took a sip of Muscadet, "yes," while sitting on a bar stool in a French restaurant on a Tuesday evening in mid-April, "Do you know it?" Janet had been talking to the owner, Pascal, about the unseasonably warm weather when Mark sat down next to her. He added, "I guess there aren't many places to stay in Beacon yet," as an elderly man with a leggy blonde on his arm entered the restaurant. She watched Pascal welcome the couple with the same familiarity he had greeted her with and then seat them by the bay window overlooking the flowering dogwoods before turning to Mark and asking, "So let me guess, you just robbed a bank and need an alibi?"

The train pulled out of Garrison and picked up speed as Janet regarded the front page of the *Times* in her hands **US Troops In Iraq Meet Fury And Gratitude** while the female conductor announced the next station over the loudspeakers. She examined the color picture of two rebels brandishing AK-47's while standing in front of a burning Humvee. The subdued play of sunlight on the water and a heron taking flight. *Members of a rebel militia, top, burned an American Humvee yesterday in Kuta, Iraq.* A red and black tugboat pushed an empty barge northward as its wake gradually moved toward the shore. *Two Americans were wounded.* The color picture of an elderly man in a turban kissing the hand of a young desert-camouflage clad GI. *In Falluja, right, an Iraqi thanked Cpl. Joseph Sharp after he and other Marines delivered food and water to civilians.* Shadows stretched across the Hudson as clouds drifted in front of the sun. *American officials agreed to call off an offensive in Falluja if local leaders can persuade guerrillas to turn in their heavy weapons.* The conductor stepped down the aisle while removing ticket stubs from the blue vinyl seats *127 Hurt As Train Hits Another Near Penn Station* and reminded Janet that her stop was next. The color picture of commuters lying on stretchers while EMS workers attend to them above the caption *Emergency teams set up a triage area in Penn Station yesterday as injured passengers awaited ambulances* as the man on his cell phone seated behind Janet insisted that his boss never had the ability to listen. *An empty Amtrak train crashed into the back of a Long Island Railroad train full of commuters about a half mile short of Pennsylvania station yesterday morning hurling passengers down aisles or into the seats in front of them and injuring 127, the authorities said.* She folded the paper in half and placed it on the aisle seat as the man behind her continued complaining.

Mark regarded Janet as she became yet another person subjected to his convoluted predicaments, "I was supposed to be meeting a client and his wife went into labor on my way up here," with a weary nod to his cell phone on the bar between them, "of course my secretary didn't bother relating the message until I got here." She was wearing a short pleated gray skirt, a semi-transparent black blouse, "well," and a pair of black knee-high boots, "that sounds like a reasonable excuse to me." He nodded thoughtfully, "let's hope all his capital doesn't wind up in her college fund." "Oh," her warm smile, "it's a girl?" "Who knows... there's a fifty-fifty chance," gently rapping his broad knuckles on the bar, "assuming it wasn't a blatant lie. Anyway that's how I ended up here." The doubts and presumptions that had made her anxious, "well," the way hunger and fatigue often did, "it might be the perfect excuse for us to have dinner together," had begun to dissipate, "that is if you—" "—That sounds great," he interjected with a grin, "my name is Mark." They shook hands. "I'm Janet." He looked closely at her dark brown eyes, "it's a pleasure to meet you." She smiled, "Likewise," before noticing that her glass was nearly empty, "So what are you investing in?"

Janet crossed to the sleigh bed, sat on the edge of it and removed her boots. A framed reproduction of Sanford R. Gifford's "Hook Mountain, near Nyack, on the Hudson" was hanging on the wall above the maple roll-top desk. She pulled down her stockings and tugged them off her feet before standing to step out of her skirt. The perspective in the painting was from the eastern shore near Croton-on-Hudson where the Metro North station was now located. She crossed to the chair in front of the desk while unbuttoning her blouse. The late September woods reached the bended shore in the foreground as the still river proceeded between a thicket of trees on the right while the mountain range in the distance blended into the yellowing horizon. The clothes she draped over the back of the chair were the only ones she brought to wear. Four sailboats and a steamer were suspended in Hook Mountain's distant reflection. She turned back the patchwork quilt and lay beneath the covers. A cloudless, cerulean blue sky mirrored the river beneath it. The smell of recently laundered sheets mingled with the perfume on her neck and perspiration beneath her arms. She thought of the conversation she had with Cindy the night before while adjusting the thick feather pillow. They cautiously discussed Cindy's decision to have lunch with Andrew and what she should wear. The warm breeze scattered dust motes away from the sunlit window as she closed her eyes and listened to the southbound train arriving, and then departing, the nearby station. Janet recalled the awkward exchange with the locksmith who arrived just minutes after Cindy had left, as he changed the locks, and then presented her with a new set of keys. She frantically packed Cindy's suitcase and left it outside the front door before catching a cab to Grand Central.

Pascal walked behind the bar, "your table will be ready in a moment." Janet smiled, "make it for two Pascal," with a nod to Mark, "he'll be joining me." Pascal shrugged, "not a problem," with a slight indulgent smile. Mark cleared his throat, "Can we get another round while we're waiting," then added a belated, "please." "Of course..." Pascal nodded, "another glass of Muscadet," then turned to Mark, "and a?" He pushed the highball glass with a half-inch of melting ice, "Dewars and soda," across the bar. "Certainly." Mark turned to Janet and asked, "So why the need for a change of scenery?" "Spring is in the air," Janet watched the clear white wine being poured, "and I've got a sentimental attachment to this town." There was the sound of dinner plates being stacked as the kitchen door swung open and then closed behind the young waiter who quickly walked past them. "But you didn't grow up around here?" Janet shook her head, "no I didn't," as the blonde woman in the dining room laughed. Mark interjected a smile into his observation, "I didn't think so." Janet added, "and neither did Pascal," as he placed the drink on the coaster in front of Mark with a curt nod and then attended to the couple seated in the dining room. Warmth flooded her thighs, "although sometimes," as she claimed, "I wish I had." Mark tasted his drink before asking, "What's that?" "Grown up here… where are you from?" "Long Island." "Perhaps you should open that hotel in Beacon." Placing his glass on the coaster, "So you'll have another place to stay the next time you need a change of scenery?" Françoise Hardy continued singing on the small speakers built into the ceiling above the bar as Janet claimed, "sometimes change can be a very good thing."

Janet stood beneath the awning in her beige raincoat as Mark drove up to the restaurant. She opened the door, "what a beautiful car," and sat down. "Thank you." The seatbelt slid across her chest as they pulled away from the curb. "Should we try and find a bar?" Janet leaned back, "I don't want to get drunk," already tipsy from the bottle of Échezeaux they had with dinner, "let's go somewhere quiet where we can watch the river." Gently stepping on the brake before the intersection, "In the car?" She nodded, "Is that okay?" He looked left and then right before taking his foot off the brake. The black BMW turned left, "there is an overlook in the park," onto the two-lane street. Victorian houses with darkened windows and tree filled yards, white picket fences, "How would you know about that?" and telephone poles slipped past. He lowered the front windows about six inches, "that's where I turned around... after I got the message that my client was driving his wife to the hospital," and the spring air mingled with the leather interior. "I think you should give your secretary a raise." The digital speedometer on the dashboard climbed as he responded, "I was going to drive back to Manhattan," while thinking about the condoms in the glove compartment. "Well," resting her hands, "I'm happy you decided to stop on your way back," on the black purse in her lap. Gripping the steering wheel, "Do you want music?" "I don't know..." she pressed her knees together, "what sort of music do you listen to?" They drove past a black and white sign indicating the posted speed.

Janet was lying on her back, "Why are you leaving," as a pair of headlights crossed her bedroom ceiling, "if she isn't coming back until Tuesday?" Mark stepped into the legs, "because I've got to," of his designer jeans, "that's why." "Well," Janet sighed, "thanks for stopping by." "Listen I'm sorry," he adjusted his belt in the dim light from the half-open window, "I've got to go." She rolled onto her side, "At four-o'clock in the morning?" and rested her forehead in the palm of her left hand. He glanced at the faint blue dial on his diving watch, "it's three-thirty," a gift from her, "I should have left hours ago," that he'd been reluctant to accept until she told him how much it cost. "Isn't today a holiday?" She persisted as he reached for his shirt, "stay with me please...you just said—" "I've got to be out there," he pushed his arms through the sleeves, "by nine," and buttoned it up. "Stay with me," they were both embarrassed by, "stay with me until I fall asleep," her urgency. Shoving in the tails, "I've got to go uptown and shower." She made a face, "mine works too you know." He stepped into his shoes before leaning over the bed, "then walk Bruno," and kissed her on the mouth. Turning her head away from his wet lips, "I hope he shits on your rug." He walked out of the bedroom, "I'll call you." She said, "don't bother," as he crossed her living room. The front door slammed and then his rapid footfalls descended the flight of stairs. She swung her legs off the bed and crossed to the window as he bounded off the stoop just in time to wave down a passing cab.

A breeze from the open window chilled the sweat on her chest and thighs as the cab sped away. The yellow glow from the streetlight pooled on the pavement and on the hoods of the parked cars. Janet turned away from the window and discovered Esther on the end of the bed diligently licking her bushy tail. She took her camisole off a pillow and put it on while walking into the living room. After turning the locks and sliding the brass chain onto the door, she removed her makeup in the bathroom mirror. Two damp cotton balls smeared with pale foundation were tossed into the empty metal garbage can beneath the sink. Sitting on the toilet seat and wiping off his semen with a wad of toilet paper before peeing. She looked down at her pale feet and dark red toenails on the black and white tiles.

Janet pulled back the top sheet and lay on the bed before pointing the remote at the television. As she adjusted the pillows behind her shoulders a terse male voice recounted the three-day hostage crisis in Beslan accompanied by a video clip of a lifeless girl in the arms of her weeping mother. She turned to a beach-front infomercial pitching energy boosting vitamin supplements, then to a music video with synchronized animated torsos gyrating in time to pulsating techno, then to handheld video footage of a massive RNC demonstration interspersed with scenes from Bush's acceptance speech, before turning the television off.

An Older Lover —Act 1

"You know my roommate is out of town," he shifted in the seat, "So maybe we can skip that play and go back to my apartment?" She placed her napkin on the table, "you said that you wanted to see it." He raised his hands, "it's probably going to be very," and flexed his middle and index fingers back and forth to quote the word, "experimental." She giggled, "Don't you mean pretentious?" "Exactly." Her thin pale arms were resting at her sides, "Is that why it's in a gallery and not in a theater?" "Most likely," he stuck out his chest, "I really just wanted to meet the writer because he edits the fiction for a monthly magazine and I wanted to give him a copy of that story I gave you last week." She nodded, "that will help him put a face to your name so—" "Yeah," he interjected, "but what if the play is terrible—" "— It's important that we go and put in an appearance at the very least." While scratching his chin, "we can always sneak out during the intermission." She pressed her palms together, "besides," while interweaving her long thin fingers, "my bed is much larger than yours." The couple seated across from them had just been served dessert. "How would you know that?" With a smile, "I think it's a safe assumption," as she placed the tip of her pointed shoe along his ankle, "and wouldn't it be more interesting for you to find out for yourself ... Mr. Intrusive?" He nodded, "let's definitely leave at intermission." She looked at his eyes while saying, "You know I really like that short story you gave me last week." The story of the married architect (played by their waiter) who is having an affair with a young woman (played by the striking hostess who seated them) that he met on a Friday afternoon in early June of '01. She blinked twice, "Is it true?" They were on their lunch hour. "Sort of," he shrugged, "I mean I took the idea from something that," then cleared his throat, "almost happened to someone I didn't know very well." The young woman was treating herself, with her first real paycheck in months, to a new pair of shoes. Raising her eyebrows, "Who?" The married architect was on his way to the bistro on the corner for a light lunch. Placing the napkin on the table, "the close friend of a friend of my," then rubbed his clammy palms on his knees, "ex-girlfriend." Sunlight warmed her legs as she sat before a broad storefront window on Mercer Street. She sounded both defensive and jealous while asking, "That actress?" The architect pocketed his wedding band while pacing the worn granite sidewalk. The waiter crossed in front of the audience on cue and presented her with the bill, "here you are," before returning to his seat in the front row. Her long auburn hair fell onto her shoulders as she leaned forward to try on a pair of shoes. "I've got it," he claimed. She walked out of the store with her purchase beneath her right arm. Taking her wallet out of the black purse, "now don't be silly it's on me," that was hanging over the back of the metal chair, "remember this was my idea." He had spent hours crafting the concisely written dialogue between the architect and the young woman as he convinced her to join him for lunch and their conversation over a shared salad niçoise and a bottle of Alsatian pinot blanc. "Well," leaning back in the seat, "how much is it?" She gave him her phone number as they walked back to the building on Broadway where she was temping. She examined the bill, "it's a bit pricey considering the quality of the ingredients," in her right hand while muttering, "but don't worry about that." The affair was passionate and lasted until the end of August. He began to blush, "I'll pay for the play," as a sheepish grin covered his face. Dinners in posh restaurants, afternoon rendezvous in her Jackson Heights apartment and one weekend in East Hampton. "And the wine was," she looked at him closely, "how many glasses did you have?" She discovered that she was pregnant in mid-August. "As many as you did," he held up the first three fingers of his right hand, "it was very good." The second act of the play *An Older Lover* portrayed their last meeting on a Friday afternoon in early September. Placing her gold American Express Card beneath the bill, "it was twelve dollars a glass." On a bench in Bowling Green Park, she offered her pregnancy and their relationship as a solution to his unhappy marriage. "Usually I don't drink wine," he drummed his fingers on the table, "but that was great," and looked around the dining room before adding the rest of his line, "Why would he give you the bill anyway?" He refused her proposition and she decided to get an abortion as soon as possible. She wondered how he would thank her for dinner, "because I was the one who asked for it." She made arrangements to get to the office a few hours early the following Tuesday in order to leave by noon for her one o'clock appointment at Planned Parenthood. He frowned before asking, "Don't you think that's rude?" She died in a cubicle when the American Airlines flight-number eleven from Boston with eighty-one passengers and eleven crew members aboard was flown into the north tower of the World Trade Center. Cindy's wire-bound notebook was closed on her lap and the ballpoint pen was tucked between the pages. "It might be a French restaurant," she admonished him sweetly, "but we're not in France." I nudged Cindy with my left elbow. He nodded, "I guess we should—" As she interjected, "are you still…" Cindy returned my smile with a wink before looking back at the stage. "I'm sorry, what were you going to say?" While the lights slowly faded to black. "No, you go ahead."

First Friday in June

Stephanie and Karen were drinking Frascati while seated at Karen's kitchen table. She lived in a railroad apartment across the street from the Greenpoint branch of the Brooklyn Public Library. Karen was a painter who'd just been dropped by her gallery and that disappointment had nagged at their conversation over dinner. Stephanie and Karen were close friends, partially because Stephanie wasn't an artist, and she was one of the least cynical people that Karen knew. What was left of the grilled chicken and asparagus pasta remained on the mismatched plates before them. The yellow linoleum floor glowed beneath the circular fluorescent light in the center of the high ceiling. A framed reproduction of Bruegel's "The Tower of Babel" hung on the wall above the green Formica table. "So what was he like," Karen placed her glass on the table, "your architect?" Stephanie winced with a grin, "he was really charming," and her enthusiasm was still blushingly obvious. Karen nodded encouragingly, "that sounds like a lot of fun." "And smart…" Stephanie didn't need much encouragement, "not self-consciously smart, but *really* smart." Karen was tired of listening to her own litany of complaints, "Was it romantic?" Stephanie thought of the man who had chatted her up on a Soho street corner, "we had a bottle of wine with lunch as well," closed her eyes and claimed, "he is so, like, drop-dead gorgeous," then picked up her glass, "but it would be just too weird," and sipped her fruity white wine. Karen leaned back in the chair, "you just said that you liked impulsive people." Stephanie exclaimed, "I said I liked spontaneous people," with a forced laugh. "No," Karen pointed at her, "*you* said impulsive." "Well," Stephanie was still a bit tipsy from her lunch with Alan when Karen opened the bottle of Frascati, "I meant to say spontaneous…" and her initial conversation with Alan, "in a Cary Grant kind of way…" reappeared in vibrantly contrasting fragments, "besides he's married." Karen shook her head, "men can be so fucking stupid." Stephanie frowned, "of course he's married," while examining the strands of pasta, "and it was all pretty brazen on his part," slivers of garlic and blots of greenish olive oil on her plate, "as well as mine for going along with it," then looked over at Karen and quietly asked, "Are you feeling any better?" The water dripping from the kitchen faucet had filled the saucepan in the bottom of the sink. Karen ignored her question, "Do you think he'll call you," while thinking about the video artist that she had been dating for a month, "or do you think that," and who had stopped returning her calls last week, "seeing him once is going to be enough?" Stephanie noted her sullen expression, "I take it that you don't want to talk about it any more." Karen topped off her glass with the rest of the wine before asking, "How old is he?" Stephanie hadn't been involved with anyone since her fiancé abruptly ended their five-year relationship the year prior, claiming that he needed to be closer to his family, and moved back to London. Since then she hadn't met anyone interesting and hadn't really been dating. "Your age I guess," Stephanie considered Karen's reaction before quietly adding, "and his wife just had a baby." "Ewww," Karen made a face, "he's just another creep!" "I know," Stephanie held up her hands, "I know," and grinned, "that was when it got really weird!" Karen prodded her, "A boy or a girl?" Stephanie sighed, "a girl… she's three-months old," with a skewed smile, "and no he didn't break out the photo album." Karen nodded, "and he's loaded," then coolly concluded, "unhappily married and rich." "He didn't seem all that unhappy to me," she defensively stated. Karen regarded Stephanie's dark brown eyes, "well," bordered by long black lashes, "there's obviously something seriously wrong with him," her full unpainted mouth, "or it's just some weird Oedipal thing," and her thick wavy hair that she dyed with henna at least once a month, "So why did you go along with it?" "He made me laugh a lot," Stephanie scratched her upper left arm, "and besides, the kid thing was initially left out," then studied her fingernails before asking, "And how is that Oedipal when he is older than me?" Karen shrugged, "maybe you look like his mother when he was a boy," as her speculative tone grew condescending, "and he was jealous of his younger sister." Stephanie rolled her eyes, "I can see those therapy sessions are finally starting to pay off," and rested her elbows on the table. "It's good to know that I'm finally getting my money's worth," Karen grinned, "you know I heard a really funny joke in therapy yesterday." She tried to remember Alan's last name while asking, "Oh really?" "I'll tell you later," with a dismissive wave of her hand, "You're not going to call him are you?"

A block of diffused sunlight warmed Stephanie's legs as she sat before the broad storefront window and removed the pair of blue satin open-toed heels from the black shoebox. "No," she took her glass off the table, "no way," and finished her wine. Her long auburn hair fell onto her shoulders as she slid her bare feet into the shoes and then carefully buckled up the thin ankle straps. "It would make your summer a bit more interesting," Karen prodded her with raised eyebrows, "and how many months has it been since…" She blushed again, "you're terrible," before quietly conceding, "nine months." Stephanie stood and walked toward the full-length mirror, "but maybe all this means is that," the shoes looked even better on her than they had in the window, "something good will finally happen." "You're looking fine with the weight you've lost," Karen smiled, "and as far as distractions go this one would rate pretty high." "Would you ever get involved with a married man?" Stephanie asked. She was framed in the tall mirror, wearing a knee-length black cotton skirt and a light blue blouse that was almost the same color as the shoes. The crowded showroom with thumping techno served as an animated backdrop. "I might now that, that video boy, has unofficially bitten the dust," Karen grinned mischievously, "What was the architect's name?" A Deer Park truck came to a grinding stop alongside the curb just outside the window. Stephanie noticed the man staring at her in the mirror, "his name is Alan," as he stood on the sidewalk, "he's Jewish as well…" and smiled at his reflection, "tall and dark with beautiful skin." Alan turned away from the window to remove his wedding band and watched a wiry Puerto Rican load four eighteen-liter water bottles onto a hand-truck.

Karen placed her elbows on the table, "*And* you got new shoes?" Stephanie removed her purse from the back of the chair, "the shoes are on my Visa," took a check for two-hundred dollars out of her wallet, "and this is for you," and handed it to Karen, "thanks again for the loan." She studied him in the mirror and decided that he resembled a younger version of that actor who became famous by playing the role of a successful surgeon on television. Karen looked at the date on the check, "Do you need me to hold this for you?" Alan sunk his hands into the front pockets of his black jeans as the water bottles were wheeled down the street. The money Stephanie owed Karen and the two thousand dollars she owed her father had been accumulated over her three-month stretch of unemployment. "I can hold it for a few weeks." "No," Stephanie shook her head, "thanks though," and smiled, "you know that the only good thing about working again is getting paid." The crunching sound of the credit card machine processing her purchase accompanied the realization that she had just charged a months worth of groceries and that yesterday she had fourteen dollars left in her checking account. Karen frowned, "but this job is only going to last for another six weeks." "Mid-July," Stephanie sighed, "don't worry," before wondering, "they really like me at the agency," if Alan would call her, "and besides I really needed a new pair of shoes."

She walked out of the store while clutching the clear plastic bag in her left hand. "Hello there," he removed his hands from his pockets, "I wouldn't normally do this," and glanced at the watch on his left wrist, "but you look very familiar," as if he'd been expecting her, "we've met before," then studied her eyes for a reassuring sign, "Haven't we?" "No," she shook her head, "I don't think so," while trying to decide if she should walk around him, "and I would have remembered," because she *hated* being accosted on the street, "if we had," though he was very handsome. He stepped toward her, "Maybe out at Montauk last August?" inadvertently blocking her path. She gave him a charitable, "that isn't very likely," yet dismissive smile. "I mean," he looked fleetingly at her legs, "and this might sound weird, and I wouldn't want you to take it the wrong way, but you look a lot like a woman that I was once very close to," and then eyed her mouth, "if you know what I mean." "I think so," she glanced at his left hand, "but, I was only out there once and that was years ago," and missed the faint tan line on his ring finger. "You're certainly not the sort of woman that should be approached on the street," sincerity coated his tone, "but, it was the only way I could speak to you." She playfully suggested, "you could have asked me for directions." The sleeves of his light green designer shirt were rolled up past his elbows, "that hardly seems plausible," and exposed his muscular forearms, "and it isn't very original." "It doesn't happen to me all that often anymore," she stated before suggesting "but you could have asked me for the time." "You aren't wearing a watch," he conceded the obvious with a nod and extended his right hand, "I'm Alan." She offered hers, "I'm Stephanie." The firmness of his grip, "it's a pleasure," on the softness of her palm, "So how would I get to Central Park from here?" She wasn't sure if he was serious, "hail a cab on the corner," and quickly decided that he wasn't. He looked over her shoulder, "Which one?" She laughed, "on Broadway

I guess," while letting go of his hand. He cleared his throat, "Can I take you to lunch?" "I don't know," she was daunted by his audacity, "and what sort of type," yet admired his courage, "might I resemble the most?" The Puerto Rican reappeared wheeling four empty bottles along the sidewalk. "That's a difficult question." Two nearly identical blondes wearing mirrored sunglasses walked by. "How so?" He slowly rubbed his hands together, "based upon my initial impression," as if to warm them, "and your exquisite taste in footwear," before thoughtfully adding, "I'd have to say for now that it isn't one type in particular but rather a composite." Disco from the open windows of a passing car accompanied her question, "Do you have a shoe fetish Alan?" "I'm afraid that I do and *you* have beautiful legs, but, this is hardly the place to confess it." "That's okay," she smiled, "most men have a fetish or two." The truck pulled away from the curb. "But my lack of a real definition clearly warrants a closer inspection." She raised her eyebrows, "Over lunch?" "Exactly... are you interested?" She transferred the shopping bag from her left to right hand, "Yes I am," then added, "although I need to be getting back to the office in about... what time is it?" He looked at his watch again, "it's a quarter past twelve." She bit her lower lip, "in another forty-five minutes," as they began walking toward the corner, "that doesn't give us very much time." "We can make it Stephanie," his forearm brushed her hip, "it's only a few blocks away."

It was a quarter till ten as Stephanie and Karen walked along the sidewalk by McCarren Park. "So this little old lady buys a vase at the thrift store and takes it home." An orange half-moon was visible between the patches of clouds. "And when she dusts it off a genie appears." The leaves on the broad plane trees lining Bedford Avenue rustled in the humid breeze. "The genie thanks her for freeing him from the vase and then grants her three wishes." The crowds gathered around the well-lit baseball diamond were watching a night game. "She says that she wants to be rich." The cracking sound of a wooden bat as it connected with a fastball that sailed deep into left field. "Poof… she is rich." Stephanie watched the ball being caught by the outfielder. "She says that she wants to live in a palace." He threw the ball to the shortstop and that kept the runner on second from tagging up. "Poof… her dingy apartment is transformed into a beautiful palace." The shortstop threw the ball to the pitcher. "And for my third and final wish I want my cat turned into a handsome prince." The pitcher inspected the ball while the next batter walked toward the plate. "And poof… wish number three transforms her mangy old tomcat into a handsome prince." The pitcher threw another fastball that the batter swung at and missed. "They fall into each others arms and then her handsome prince asks, 'So aren't you sorry that you had me fixed?' "

A livery cab finally took Stephanie back to Jackson Heights around two in the morning. "I hope that I didn't get you into trouble this afternoon," she stood before the answering machine in her living room, "and I really enjoyed our lunch together," swaying a bit from the Mojitos she had with Karen at Pete's Candy Store, "and I'd like to do it again…" with glistening eyes and a broad smile, "that is if you want to," and listened to his message three more times, "call me at this number or at my office tomorrow," before turning out the lights and crawling into bed, "I'll be working till the late afternoon."

Audition Sequence

I locked my bike up to a parking meter in front of the gallery and pocketed the keys. Cindy removed the highlighted script from her purse as the F train pulled out of York Street. It was a warm, partly cloudy Sunday morning. She opened the script and turned to page nine.

                         Man:
            And what about the guy she's with?

A flock of pigeons had surrounded a crushed loaf of bread in the gutter between two parked cars.

                        Woman:
        He is nothing more than the latest way for her to
                      wear her hair.

Peter was standing in front of the gallery with a copy of the Sunday *Times* tucked beneath his left arm and a hand-rolled cigarette between his fingers.

                         Man:
                     And for him?

Peter had been a member of the Living Theater in the late sixties, "Hey Donald," spent most of the seventies in Rome, "nice day for a ride," and now owned the gallery where the play was performed, "Did you take the Manhattan Bridge?"

                        Woman:
        She is nothing more than a new pair of shoes.

Cindy was reminded of meeting Janet for the first time, dressed in a beige raincoat and holding a small red umbrella above her head, as she stood in front of the fountain by the Met on a drizzling March afternoon.

```
                          Man:
        Are you sure that you're not projecting your own
                       insecurities?
```

I nodded, "there was hardly any traffic."

Cindy looked up from the script and out the keyed window—**Part marsupial part lynx:** *Seeking an affectionate femme who doesn't take herself too seriously, likes art and loves cats. I am hoping to share spring blossoms with someone like you if the glass slipper fits.* After a brief tour of the modern wing Cindy and Janet had an intimate conversation over tea and cake in the museum café.

Peter's long gray hair was tied back in a loose ponytail, "so, that's why you're early." I stepped toward him, "I'm always early," while undoing the chinstrap on my helmet, "it's one of my compulsions." The photograph of a long row of American flags flying above yesterday's memorial ceremony at the World Trade Center site was partially obscured by his thin wrist. "That isn't a bad compulsion to have," Peter grinned. I removed my helmet and tucked it beneath my left arm. "So we'll be able to rehearse here as well?" "Sure," He pushed the thin wire frames up his nose, "we close at seven so you can use the space anytime after that." The street was faintly reflected in the gallery's front window. "You shouldn't have any problems," taking a drag off his cigarette, "except for that opening on the second Friday in October," he exhaled, "you missed the opening for this show." I thought of the grainy black and white postcard of a dilapidated house surrounded by bare trees that came in the mail a few weeks ago, "we had a production meeting," and was now stuck on my refrigerator door. "The show in October is photography as well... just work on the walls."

Cindy recalled her walk through the West Village last April, following a depressing lunch with Andrew, the afternoon when she finally told him that she was living with a woman. Cindy climbed the stairs and saw her bulky suitcase outside Janet's door— she tried the locks (with the keys she'd been given just two weeks ago) and discovered that they had been changed. She dialed Janet's number on her cell phone, listened to the phone ringing on the other side of the door, hung up when the answering machine instructed her to leave a message and then dragged her suitcase down the narrow flight of stairs. She sat on the stoop and checked the messages on her phone. Janet had called from Grand Central to inform Cindy that she was spending the rest of the week in the Berkshires with an old friend, she was very sorry to end things this way and that was followed by an exasperated sigh. Janet said that she would feel really terrible if changing the locks had hurt her but she simply hated to make a scene. Janet wished her luck and then made a point of not saying goodbye before hanging up. Cindy sat on the stoop while trying to decide if she should wait around (not believing the rest of the week in the Berkshires lie) or take a cab back to Brooklyn.

                         Woman:
                       Sweetheart...

She roused herself off the stoop after the downstairs neighbor walked past her with a knowing smirk, entered the building and let the heavy door slam behind him.

...I didn't mean anything by that.

"It's not much of a set anyway," I watched a small barking dog being lead by an elderly Hispanic woman pass by while adding, "it's just two folding chairs and a pair of speakers."

                         Man:
                         Oh no?

Cindy hauled her suitcase to the curb and hailed a cab.

                       Woman:
         No, absolutely not... all of the things that
      were important to me then seem so superficial...
                    especially now...

The ride over the Manhattan Bridge in a cab, her third that day, took longer than the subway because of the rush-hour traffic.

        ...although all of those encounters became
                      relationships.

"You've got to tell me when you'll need the space," Peter tapped the ash off his cigarette, "and I'll be around to lock up when you're done," before taking another drag. "I should have a better idea after the auditions." "How long will you need the gallery today?" he asked.

Andrew couldn't hide his astonishment when Cindy rang the bell and asked him to come downstairs and give her a hand with the suitcase.

I scratched my chin, "one o'clock, we shouldn't run any later than that today." Peter glanced at his watch, "And the performances are at the end of October?"

Man:
Would you like to go somewhere else after dinner,
instead of that play?

"The Friday and Saturday before Halloween. And the show is just over an hour long."

Woman:
No, why do you ask?

Andrew spent the rest of the night assuring Cindy that she had made the right decision, that things would definitely be different this time, that he would finally cut back on his drinking and that they should seriously consider couples therapy.

Woman:
Please don't mope, I find that so unappealing.

Cindy didn't have the courage to tell him why she really came back and it didn't come up until their first big fight a month later.

Man:
Then why did you say that?

Peter turned to me and asked, "And you're turning this play into a novel?"

Woman:
You're being so sensitive.

"There isn't really going to be any play... it's all fiction."

Man:
All of my questions, some people think that I am
very intrusive.

He furrowed his brow, "Oh really?"

Woman:
No sweetheart, besides how else will we get to
know each other?

I tried to elaborate, "the novel is loosely based on the production of a performance that never happened."

Man:
I just don't want you to think that I'm using you.

Flicking his cigarette over the curb, "So I'm a character in it as well?"

Woman:
I don't, and I'm not…

I said, "we are all characters in this book."

and I'll never… I swear.

Cindy slid the script into her purse as the train slowed before the station. Peter shook his head, "So I'm the eccentric ex-hippie who owns the gallery where the play, that isn't really a play, takes place?" She stood up as the doors opened. "Am I correct in assuming that this is only a minor role?" And walked along the platform as the F train pulled out of the station. "If there is such a thing." She climbed the stairs behind a young couple. His eyes narrowed, "Can you give me twenty a week to use it as your rehearsal space?" The sun gradually emerged from behind a bank of clouds as Cindy reached the top of the stairs. "Sure... I can give you twenty now if you want." Cindy waited on the corner of Delancy and Essex for the light to change. "Good," Peter nodded, "and don't leave a mess when you're done." A silver SUV moved through the intersection after the light turned green. I opened my wallet, "I'll make sure that doesn't happen," took out a twenty and handed it to him. She crossed the street along with an elderly man holding his granddaughter's hand. Peter looked over my shoulder, "Isn't that your director?" The two men standing beside the bodega drinking beer out of paper bags watched Cindy walk by. I turned around, "yeah," and Cindy nodded while passing the fire hydrant, "How did you know that?" He shrugged, "she came by the other day," then lowered his voice, "you know I really liked your last book." "Thanks." "But this seems really self-indulgent," he put the twenty in his wallet, " and I *really* don't like the idea of being one of your characters." "Hey Cindy," I smiled, "this is Peter." "Hello again," she shook his hand. "He lives upstairs and runs the gallery." "Yeah I know..." she turned to me, "I came by last Thursday when the photographer was hanging her show."

Peter unlocked the door and set his newspaper on the windowsill before turning on the lights, "here we are." The gallery had a high ceiling, a polished hardwood floor and rows of framed black and white photographs hanging on the walls. He crossed to the rear of the gallery, "let me get you some chairs," and slid open a tall white door. I stood before the photograph that had been reproduced for the postcard and noticed three crows in the overgrown yard. He came out of the office with two metal chairs and asked, "So this is your set?" Cindy unfolded both chairs before sitting down. He crossed the gallery, "I'm meeting some collectors for lunch," took his paper from the window-sill, "so I'll leave you to your audition." "See you around," I said as the door closed behind him.

Cindy removed her copy of the script and a manila file filled with headshots from her purse. I walked across the gallery and sat in the opposite chair, "we can rehearse here anytime after seven." She was thumbing through the pictures in her lap, "How much is that going to cost?" "Don't worry about it." "Why," with a grin, "did you just win the lottery?" "No, I'm tapping into my trust fund." She crossed her legs, "I bet you say that to all the girls." "Only the ones I'm trying to sleep with." She handed me a photograph, "here's that picture of Elizabeth," of an attractive middle-aged woman with shoulder length brown hair and dark brown eyes, "she's the one I have in mind for the woman in the first act." I turned the picture over, "Whoa…" and skimmed her extensive resume, "she was Petra in *The Bitter Tears of Petra von Kant*," then looked up at Cindy, "I wish I could have seen that staged… the film is in my all time top five." "I spoke to her yesterday and she said that she'd be here early," Cindy smiled, "she's probably on her way right now."

Elizabeth hailed a cab on the corner of Broadway and 13th street. She opened the rear door before the cab came to a complete stop. She gave the driver the gallery's address while pulling the seatbelt across her chest. The rear windows were halfway down and the warm air blowing through them smelled faintly of the ocean. The driver glanced at her in the rearview mirror after they sped past two black men wearing tuxedos riding a tandem bike. The cab slowed before the intersection at Houston and then made a left after the light turned green.

"I was thinking about your script on the train," Cindy frowned, "about the way people consume others simply for the sake of the experience." I looked at her closely, "You mean as an extension of themselves?" "Just for the experience," she nodded, "and then they just get cast aside when it's over," before looking intently at the floor, "I was in love with a woman a lot like the one in the first act." "Me too," I admitted before asking, "Was she an actress?"

Third Friday in June

"I haven't been out here in years," Alan parked the Range Rover, "no it was decades ago," then pulled the key out of the ignition. Stephanie turned to him, "On a field trip?" He glanced at his watch, "exactly," and decided that at that moment his wife was either nursing Olivia or looking on while their new West Indian nanny changed another diaper, "it might have been in the fifth grade." They opened their doors and stepped onto the pavement while he added, "when the dinosaurs were still roaming the planet." "You're only five years older than me," Stephanie closed her door, "I don't know why you need to make such a big deal about it," and fixed her bangs in the tinted window. "That may be true," Alan activated the alarm before pocketing the keys, "but it seems like ancient history." She was wearing an orange summer dress, "oh you poor baby," and her new blue satin heels, "Did you sneak out of work just to feel sorry for yourself?" His anxiety dissolved with the realization that the chances of being discovered at the Queens Museum on a Friday afternoon with this beautiful young woman, "I'm not begrudging your, so called freedom," were almost as great as being struck by a meteorite, "and I'm honored that you're willing to share some of it with me." She took his hand while saying, "let's make the most of the time we have together," as they began walking across the parking lot. The sound of her heels on the pavement and the sight of her beautiful pale feet offset by the sparkling iridescent blue polish on her toenails, "I remember having a lot of fun," and her exquisitely turned ankles had eradicated the host of implausible explanations coursing through his head, "on that field trip," in the unlikely event that Elaine would interrogate his secretary after being unable to reach him on his cell phone. A group of adults in matching green T-shirts and grey sweat pants were being helped aboard an idling bus by a heavyset black man wearing a Mets cap. Stephanie looked at Alan with a smile, "I come out here on my bike all the time," as the sunlight reflecting off the nearby unisphere caused her to squint, "I really love this park." They walked along the sidewalk as starlings filled the air with their mimicry. Alan held the door for her, "after you," and watched her hips sway before him as they entered the museum. Stephanie greeted the elderly female attendant behind the counter while fishing a few quarters from her purse. The woman handed over two small green stickers and told them to have a good visit.

The desk fan on her dresser cast another wave of cool air, "I came home one afternoon," over their bare bodies, "right after they'd had another fight... their final fight," as they lay facing each other, "and the house was really quiet," with their heads resting on a pair of pillows, "in a weird way," and the white sheets, "like the way the sky is charged before a thunderstorm," were crumpled beneath them, "like if you breathe too deeply it might shock you." The drawn blinds and the late afternoon sun, "I'd usually go to the movies then... and I saw so many crappy ones," created broad streaks on the wall above her double bed, "sometimes I'd just sit in the theater and wait for the movie to start again," Stephanie turned onto her back and studied the cracks on the ceiling, "but I stayed in my room." Alan suppressed a yawn before closing his eyes. "I heard a car door slam so I went to the window and watched my father driving away." An ice cream truck slowly passed on the street below her window. "My mother started dating a few weeks later. She would bring these young guys from her office home or married men she'd meet in bars."

Alan and Stephanie stepped onto the wide, glass-bottomed balcony as the model of the city, depicting every building and roadway constructed in all five boroughs before 1992, lay sprawled before them. Thousands of multicolored building blocks rose above the vast grid-work of streets, alleyways, avenues, boulevards, and highways, dozens of skyscrapers punctuated the meticulously replicated Manhattan skyline, tiny piers jutting into the deep blue Hudson, the various shades of green plastic turf representing the city's parks and infrequent vacant lots, while the Harlem River and the East River, both painted the same unlikely deep blue, were spanned by the bridges that connected Manhattan to faithfully rendered reproductions of the Bronx, Queens, Brooklyn—and from Brooklyn to Staten Island via the replica of the Verrazano Bridge—thousands of streets and avenues, seemingly endless expressways, all bordered by thousands upon thousands of blocks of houses, storefronts, tenements, factories, housing projects, scaled mile upon mile of hilly green parks coated in various shades of green, headstone filled cemeteries, long stretches of elevated subway lines and their faithfully rendered stations, two airports, a wildlife preservation and the narrow stretches of the city's sandy beaches were all contained in this vast air-conditioned room. Stephanie was happy to be sharing the view from one of her favorite places in the city with Alan, "I'm going to kiss you all night," and squeezed his hands. He drew her closer, "I'd like that." They shared a passionate kiss as the overhead lights gradually dimmed and tiny streetlights constellated the replica of the city beneath them.

She cleared her throat, "Are you still awake?" Alan opened his eyes, "of course," and blinked twice, "it's nice just to lie here with you." Her palms were pressed on the mattress, "I thought maybe you were taking a nap." He yawned before saying, "I'm not getting very much sleep at home," and rubbed his eyes. "Because of Olivia?" He yawned again, "she has yet to sleep through the night." "I was afraid that," Stephanie turned toward him, "that I was boring you," and traced her fingers along his chin. He smiled, "no not at all." The blinds rocked in the breeze as the horizontal shadows swayed on the wall above the bed. "Yeah, but I shouldn't go on and on about my dysfunctional childhood." Alan shook his head, "it's always helpful to compare notes." She kissed his chin, "well you can come over and take a nap anytime you want." "Are you close to your father?" She thought of her father, "he's been helping me out a lot lately financially," who was most likely planted in his cubicle, "I really wish he'd remarry or at least start dating again," and working through an endless series of calculations, "What about you?" Alan yawned again before saying, "he's dead." "Oh," Stephanie clutched his arm, "I am so sorry." He was touched by her impulse, "it's okay," while thinking of the long days and nights he spent, "he lost a long fight with cancer," bedside in a private room at Sloan Kettering, "and died two years ago," eyeing the narcotic drip that invariably followed another round of chemotherapy. "Were you very close?" And after a few weeks sitting bedside at a hospice, "it was his firm," the final rainy afternoon at Union Field Cemetery with a few hundred mourners. "Do you miss him?" Alan thought of the panorama they'd strolled around a few hours ago, "he was very good at what he did," and recalled the replica of the cemetery where his father was buried, "and took pride in his work… as clichéd as that sounds." She shook her head, "it doesn't." "Most of my achievements, to a certain extent, all of my achievements are a result of his hard work… and with the exponential growth the firm is experiencing right now I can't share it with him." "Well," she quietly suggested, "he'd have a granddaughter now." "He never had time for his children," Alan concluded, "I studied architecture to be closer to him and all I've done is inherit his success."

The overhead lights came up as she whispered, "it's morning again my dear and time for me to get on the subway," then kissed him on the ear, "and go to work." He placed his hands on her shoulders, "Why don't you call in sick?" She said, "Again?" with a smile. He anticipated the rest of the afternoon in her Jackson Heights apartment, "you can do that everyday." Stephanie felt as dizzy as she sometimes did just before falling asleep, "you're going to get me fired." Alan repeated the offer, "I'll pay your rent," he had made yesterday on his cell phone while pushing Olivia in her stroller through Prospect Park. "I like my job," she squeezed his hands, "and besides I don't want a sugar daddy." He shrugged, "just for a few months." "I think you should see my place before saying that." Alan placed his hands on her shoulders, "I didn't think you were going to ask," and kissed her on the forehead. She nodded at the city behind him, "it's right over there," and pointed at Queens, "but you can't really see it from here."

Stephanie lived in a small one-bedroom apartment on the fourth floor of a five-story walk up on 76th Street near the corner of 37th Avenue. Their shoulders were resting on the headboard as she asked, "Would you like a glass of wine?" He raised his eyebrows, "sure." She swung her bare legs off the bed, "it's probably not as good as what you're used to." "I'm no snob," Alan admired her body, "and a glass of wine would be really nice," as she walked across the bedroom. "There is a liquor store around the corner," as she passed through the open door she added, "and they have a beautiful dog." "Not a great selection," he called after her, "but a beautiful dog?" She opened the refrigerator, "the selection is okay," removed the bottle of Saint-Veran from the top shelf, "I guess..." pulled out the cork, "I mean I'm no expert," and filled two juice glasses with the straw colored wine, "but the dog is very beautiful." "Hey Stephanie," he called again from the bed, "does this dog have a name?" She stood in the doorway, "yes," and took a sip from her glass, "the dog's name is Ali," before re-crossing the bedroom, "it's a German Shepherd." Alan took the glass from her and asked, "Like Mohammed Ali?" Stephanie sat on the side of the bed, "it happens to be a she." He grinned, "that's strange." "The owners are Asian," she leaned back, "so I'm sure it means something else." He tasted the wine, "this is nice." "Well," she raised her glass in a toast, "happy Father's Day."

Exclusions Apply—Part 1

"It's been such a gloomy week," Janet had her hair and nails done the day before, "it's like the entire city is in mourning again," when the maid came to clean the apartment, "not that I blame them one bit… I was so depressed on Wednesday as well." James couldn't find anywhere to put his hands, "this week has been like one long hangover," was at a loss for the right words, "before the next nightmare begins," and was annoyed that all of the things he had prepared to say evaporated just after she buzzed him into her building and he began climbing the carpeted stairs with the bouquet in his right hand, "You know what I mean?" His political banter had been tailored by time-killing conversations with his left-leaning coworkers and customers who lingered by the cash register bending his ear with impassioned attacks on the half-witted president and the neo-con goons who were running the country into the ground. He swallowed hard, "I guess I should say before the nightmare continues."

She had kissed him hungrily on the mouth when he presented her with the dark red Gerber daises and happily exclaimed that they were one of her favorites. The light green stems nestled in a few inches of cold tap water were enlarged by the cylindrical crystal and tilted away from the curved lip of the vase, making the daises look like they were bowing before, or even humbled by, her spotless brightly-lit kitchen. They were thrown away on Monday.

Janet found their conversation distracting, "Did you see Bush's acceptance speech?" James was dressed in the clothes he wore to work, "it was on the radio at the store," as he stood before her fidgeting, "I gotta man-date," while silently recalling the episodes from his adolescence that he had deemed worthy of plying her with. "I really thought Kerry was going to win," Janet walked to the refrigerator, "I didn't at first but after the debates," opened the door and produced a bottle of Veuve Cliquoit from a lower shelf, "anyway, I got this today," she held the neck of the bottle in her slender right hand while suggesting, "perhaps we can find something to celebrate." The earnest conviction that shadowed James on the F train had finally entered her kitchen, "How about the end of democracy in America?" "I'm afraid we'll have plenty of time to do that," Janet placed the bottle on the counter by the vase, "Wouldn't you rather drink to us?" He was almost comfortable enough to launch into a candid conversation about how wonderful it felt to be falling in love, "that sounds like a perfect place to start." She took two thin flutes out of the cabinet above the sink and placed them on the counter, "I'm glad you agree," then peeled back the gold foil on the bottle before loosening the wire holder and carefully twisting off the cork, "with me," a muffled pop, "everything has been dominated by the election..." was followed by the wisp of pale smoke that wavered over the open bottle, "and it is so boring." The light amber wine infused with tiny spiraling bubbles rapidly climbed the flutes and after the blooming foam gradually subsided she slowly filled them. Janet leaned forward and smiled, "come on you," before taking the bottle and her glass off the counter, "I think you'll find that the light in the living room is much more generous." "Yeah but," he grinned, "it's even better in your bedroom." Kissing him on the cheek she replied, "the night is young before it's old." He admired her walk as she crossed to the couch, "So why are Gerber daises one of your favorite flowers?" After placing the bottle on the side table she sat down, "I like how bare the stems are," leaned back and crossed her legs, "plus my hair was almost that color last spring." He studied the black and white Warhol silkscreen of Jackie Onassis hanging above the couch, "Like that actress we saw last Friday?" She grinned, "but it didn't look as cheap as her hair." The lamp beside the armchair threw his passing shadow over the painting.

First Friday in July

"When was this?" Heat vapors wavered above the yellow sand, "Monday night," as the smell of marijuana, "the day before he went away," and a faint reggae rhythm drifted by. "When was your last period?" Topless women were sprawled on colorful towels, "A few weeks ago," and groups of men wearing thongs lounged in beach chairs. A few children by the shore, "So you're probably ovulating," were playing before the breaking waves. Two women were swimming beyond the breakers while a surfer drifted past the sandbar while waiting for another ride. "Why didn't you get the morning after pill?" Stephanie and Karen were in their bikini bottoms while sitting cross-legged on a white sheet. "I didn't have the money but I'm pretty sure that I took care of it in time. " The afternoon sky was cloudless. "What do you mean, 'took care of it?'" The hazy blue line above the horizon, "I took a bunch of birth control pills the next morning," was broken by the silhouettes of two motionless oil tankers, "and I told Alan not to worry about it." Karen was livid, "that isn't like you at all," after learning that Stephanie had been let go from the temp agency last week for missing too many days, "what were you," and was spending all of her time with a married man who drank like a fish, "What *are* you thinking?" She merely shrugged, "you shouldn't worry about it either," and was reluctant to convey the growing host of doubts she had about Alan, "although at times it seems like things are happening way too fast," wary of Karen's rush to judgment, "but we came out here to relax," and afraid of her anger, "Okay?"

The box fan in her kitchen window drowned out the Stereolab CD playing in the living room. Alan signed the company check for three thousand dollars, "I know someone who may be looking for a personal assistant," and handed it to Stephanie, "but you can't sleep with him," while sitting at the table in his underwear. She took the check, "ha-ha," and glanced at the amount before folding it in half. They had just finished a bottle of Macon Villages. "I'm just joking," he rolled the pen between his palms, "besides, he's gay," and grinned. Elaine and Olivia were in Martha's Vineyard for the month, "come on, don't pout," and he was flying out the following afternoon to join them, "you aren't very sexy when you sulk," for two weeks of family vacation. Stephanie was wearing the semi-transparent pink camisole he'd just given her. She opened the utensil drawer and slipped the check into it before asking, "Are you hungry?" Melting ice filled the tall water glass on the Formica counter. He leaned back in the chair, "I'm starving," and crossed his arms over his stomach. She turned to him, "I'd cook you something but it's too hot." Two wine glasses were on the kitchen table beside the empty wine bottle with a sketch of a chateau on its beige label. "You know that I'm going to miss you." She stepped toward him, "thanks for the money," placed her hands on his shoulders, "can you call your friend before you go so I can get an interview," and kissed him on the forehead, "as soon as possible." He eyed her mouth, "Why won't you let me buy you an air conditioner?" She considered his question, "Maybe a small one for the bedroom?" Alan reached for her, "What's the matter?" She straddled him in the chair, "How could you think that I would have sex with just anyone?" "I was just joking," he pressed his face between her breasts. She bit his earlobe before whispering, "I'm not a whore."

Karen's thick cork-soled sandals were holding down two corners of the sheet, "When were you on the pill?" Stephanie's blue beach bag, "last fall," and a nearly empty plastic water bottle held down the other ends. "And he came inside you?" A pack of yellow American Spirits and a small green disposable lighter were on the sheet between them. She nodded, "twice." Karen shook her head in disbelief, "twice." Stephanie brushed a lock of hair away from her mouth, "the condom broke." A plane pulling a broad banner for a car insurance company flew past them. "I don't want to talk about it." Karen took a cigarette from the pack, "What," and placed it between her lips, "were you both drunk?" Stephanie shook her head while saying, "he'll pay for the abortion," then added, "but I really don't think I'm pregnant," with conviction. Karen lit the cigarette, "you don't know that yet." A large white seagull landed nearby and began picking at a brown paper bag. The smoke from her cigarette drifted along with the breeze. Stephanie uncrossed her legs, "if I am pregnant he'll pay for it," sank her heels into the hot sand and placed her hands on her knees. "Two condoms broke?" A black girl in a bright pink one-piece was digging a hole in the sand with a small orange shovel. "No," Stephanie shook her head, "he came twice." Karen cleared her throat before asking, "How did that happen?" The girl's father stood beside her in cut-off jeans and a sleeveless T-shirt. "Weren't you going to quit smoking?" "Yeah well," Karen clenched her jaw, "please don't try and change the subject." Stephanie said, "he'll pay for it," before looking away. The blond lifeguard continued twirling his silver whistle. "It's really too bad that he can't have the abortion for you as well." Stephanie turned to Karen, "he's getting me an interview at his friend's law firm." "Oh yeah," Karen made no effort to hide her skepticism, "And when is this going to happen?" A long wave rolled against the shore. "Pretty soon I guess." Karen tapped the ash off her cigarette, "Is this firm under Alan's desk?" "No," Stephanie shook her head, "it's at the World Trade Center," and smiled before asking, "Have you found a new gallery yet?" "No..." Karen's eyes narrowed, "Why do you need a job if he is paying your rent?" Stephanie leaned back and took her bikini top out of the beach bag, "because I don't want him to support me," that covered her breasts as she tied it on, "I'm going for a swim," then stood up, "see you later," and walked across the warm stretch of sand before the shore.

Alan and Stephanie sat across from each other at her favorite Thai restaurant. "My father was always very cautious with money and I'm not saying that there is anything wrong with that, but at times it was a real hindrance, especially when it came to some of the more ambitious projects we would bid on." The remnants of their dinner, barbequed pork and a cold duck salad, lay on the green plates. "So you don't worry about the costs at all?" "Not in the initial stages," Alan refilled his beer glass, "ultimately it comes into play but that's why engineers exist." "Do you use the same engineer for every project?" He shook his head, "it depends on the project," then drank from his glass, "our senior engineer was very close to my father and to his way of doing things," and wiped his mouth with a paper napkin, "but we rarely see eye to eye anymore." Stephanie was trying not to be distracted by the large color television behind his head, "Why wasn't your father able to turn the company around the way that you have?" There was silent footage from a congressman's news conference and a black and white still of his missing intern. "My father was too loyal to a few individuals who always insisted on doing things the same way and my main objective has always been to have a solid working relationship with the client and to really explore what their needs are. The greater an understanding I have for what they want increases the project's potential and its chances for success." A dog commercial followed. "It's the client that always comes first," Alan rested his elbows on the table, "and I'd really like to work with a younger team of engineers... who have fresh, open ideas as opposed to a few of my father's old cronies who are set in the past." She looked away from the television, "my friend Karen has a reproduction of the "Tower of Babel" in her kitchen." He blinked twice, "Have you seen the original?" "No," Stephanie shook her head, "have you?" He nodded, "it's in Vienna." "Karen lives in Greenpoint," she poked her fork into a piece of duck, "she's a really good painter." He nodded, "Where did she go to school?" She placed the duck in her mouth, "Pratt," and began to chew, "like a decade or so ago." Alan caught the waitresses' eye, "they really aren't known for their painting program," and held up the empty beer bottle. Stephanie nodded, "she's pretty frustrated right now." "Why is that?" There were scenes from a car accident behind his head and an eyewitness who used both of her hands to describe the crash. "Karen just lost her gallery." The pretty waitress appeared with another bottle of beer and took the empty away. "Because she wasn't selling?" She nodded, "I really like her work," and watched him refill his glass, "That blue painting in my living room?" He nodded, "That one of the ocean?" She smiled, "Karen painted that."

Sunlight glistened on the water as Stephanie waded in between the waist-high breakers. She dove beneath a towering wave and swam a few yards beneath the surface. She felt invigorated by the cool water while floating on her back with her arms outstretched, legs together and eyes wide open. She was nearly weightless beneath the blue sky as the ocean swayed beneath her. A plane flying out of JFK crossed the sky as her long auburn hair fanned out around her head in the dark blue water.

Exclusions Apply—Part 2

The cushion sagged beneath James as he sat down beside her, "Did you just get your hair cut?" The copy of his short story that he gave her two weeks ago, before they parted with an awkward kiss at the top of the Chambers Street station, was lying atop the October issue of French *Vogue*. "Yesterday," Janet ran her left hand through her bobbed hair, "do you like it?" Steam coursed through the radiator beneath the window. "Yeah a lot," he took a sip of champagne, "it's very sexy." The green bottle with the yellow label was beaded with condensation. She held the stem of her glass with her left index finger and thumb, "it was such a pretty day," then took a sip before adding, "I so love autumn." He stopped himself from mentioning how the afternoon and evening had dragged at the bookstore, "I prefer winter," knowing that it would bore her, "it's more austere," although he could always attribute his impatience to wanting to be with her. She listened to the sound of the wind in the trees outside the window, "winter is too dark for me," as pages of newspaper sailed down the street, "the cold doesn't bother me that much," then gestured with her right hand, "but the lack of sunlight drives me absolutely mad." Regarding the multitude of bubbles gradually climbing his glass, "What about summer?" "The absolute worst," Janet was wearing a snug low-cut gray cashmere sweater, "unless I'm away... but this city is simply insufferable then," that accentuated her narrow cleavage, "I'd have to say that spring is my favorite season," a pleated thigh-high black skirt, "but this is a close second," silver fishnets and high heels, "Are you hungry?" He shook his head, "no," and tried to think of something meaningful to say, "not really." She raised her eyebrows, "And what does that mean?" He had inhaled a medium rare cheeseburger, "I had a late lunch," while hunched over a box of books in the cluttered office, "around four." "Well, if you change your mind," rocking her right leg back and forth over her left knee, "I could order us something or we could—" He leaned over and kissed her on the mouth. "That's much better." Last Friday night, after sitting through the first act of the play, they took a cab back to her place and went straight to bed. She caressed his cheek with the palm of her right hand and kissed him. "We could just sit here and drink champagne." She had been as generous as he was eager to please, and they had lingered within the intricacies of their pleasure. "That's not what you," Janet placed her hand on his thigh, "really want to do." Her glossy lipstick left a powdery taste of violets on his mouth. "Maybe not." The conversations between couplings were a multiple exchange of carefully selected memories. "Well," she whispered in his ear, "you should always say what you mean." They finally fell asleep a few hours before dawn. James looked closely at her eyes, "And you?" She woke up alone in the mid-morning to the faint sound of the shower. Fluttering her lashes, "And me what?" Then joined him in the tiled stall where they soaped, scrubbed and rinsed each other off. James left for work an hour later.

Janet's detailed character sketch began to emerge at his desk the following morning. The afternoons at the bookstore were more tedious than usual because of Kerry's concession speech. James spent most of the nights that week lying in bed with the phone pressed to his ear, listening to nostalgic descriptions from her past, that he would rework in the morning on his laptop. On Thursday night he brought a pint of bourbon home and left a thoughtful message on her answering machine before cracking the seal. After finishing the pint he went down to the bar on the corner and described the affair he was having with a woman that he'd met at The Strand a few weeks ago. The bartender and a few of his acquaintances hunched over pints of tap beer exchanged skeptical glances. Beneath the din of The Buzzcocks' "Why Can't I Touch It?" he boasted of the great sex they'd had last Friday night. After he had rattled off a detailed inventory of the contents in her West Village apartment, the bartender—a gum chewing self-taught painter in her late twenties—asked if she owned it. He exclaimed that the apartment was just a small part of her divorce settlement. The bartender wanted to know what she did for a living. James claimed that she didn't need to work, that her second husband was some big shot CEO and still took very good care of her, to keep up appearances, James presumed, because he had recently left her for his secretary. When James returned from work on Friday night he discovered a perfumed letter in his mail box that contained a brief passage from Baudelaire (written with a fountain pen on handmade paper) and a black and white photograph of Janet when she was his age and living in Paris. He sat at his desk and assessed her youthful beauty beneath the lamp. He tacked the picture to the wall above his desk and spent the rest of the night reading Richard Howard's translation of *Les Fleurs du Mal*. He spent Saturday morning lying in bed and imagining her Parisian world—as a painter's assistant during the three years she lived there—of studios and galleries, dancing till dawn in new wave discotheques, drinking in Left Bank bars, and the array of lovers she had in addition to the German sculptor she was briefly married to. After masturbating, he showered and then shaved in the foggy mirror above the sink. The sidewalks had been swept by the wind and the blue sky was cloudless. He caught himself staring at the digital clock on the cash register an hour after he got to work. An unending line of customers who claimed that they were all going to move to Canada filled the long afternoon. He had to wait for twenty minutes on the frigid subway platform with his hands jammed in his pockets. The Gerber daisies had been purchased at the deli by the subway station and were shoved beneath his right arm as he walked up her block. He pressed the bell with his right index finger and then waited for her to buzz him in.

James gently mocked her tone, "Do you really say what you mean?" She nodded with conviction, "always." "I don't know if I believe you." Janet gave him a wounded look, "oh is that so…" while refilling their glasses. James cleared his throat, "tell me more about the director of that play we saw last week." She placed the bottle on the coaster, "Who Cindy?" He nodded, "the one you introduced me to." The hem of her skirt rose as she re-crossed her legs, "it's funny that you should mention Cindy," exposing the little black bow on her shimmering garter belt, "because she called this afternoon," and an inch of bare thigh. "It must be my precognitive powers kicking in again." Janet weighed all the time she had invested in compromised company to dull her loneliness, "or the champagne," and how often it transformed her expectations into pain, "it's gone straight to your head." "And?" Janet's hand returned to his thigh, "Cindy called to see how I was doing," and she squeezed it reassuringly, "and to tell me that she misses me," then paused briefly to gauge his response, "she also wanted to know if I liked the play." James laughed maliciously and Janet smiled with relief. "Wasn't she jealous," he sipped his champagne, "seeing us together?" Janet frowned, "I think she was confused." "What else did she say?" She conceded his question with a nod, "Cindy was afraid that the play might have offended me." James exclaimed, "so, it *was* about us." Janet rolled her eyes, "uh-huh," before taking a sip, "she said that she wanted to come by sometime soon so we could talk," and her lie was complimented by a faint blush. "When, tonight?" "Sometime soon," she looked closely at his eyes, "Cindy is a deeply unhappy person."

Janet was reminded of seeing Cindy again for the first time… a tall brunette in a knee-length black leather jacket who stepped toward her as she stood in front of the fountain by the Met on a drizzling March afternoon. They recognized each other from their online photographs and readily acknowledged that neither looked as good in pictures as they did in person. While climbing the marble steps leading to the museum entrance they talked about the miserable weather and shared subway horror stories while waiting to check their coats. After a brief tour of the modern wing—the Klee's on the mezzanine were Cindy's favorites—they spent a few hours in the café. Cindy tactfully described the deteriorating relationship she was in before claiming that it was almost over. Cindy confessed that she was still living with her boyfriend while secretly searching for a studio. Janet was tempted to offer her place as a temporary share that afternoon but waited until the following week, while they were having lunch at Pastis, before making her offer. Cindy moved in the first Wednesday in April and it took Janet just a few days to realize that she had made a serious mistake. She made no effort to find her own place and Janet was afraid that her stay was becoming indefinite. Any mention of the apartment search or finding a job was met with a scowl and hours of sullen silence. When Janet showered her with affection, Cindy confessed that she was really depressed, equated her life with nothing and tearfully apologized for being so worthless. Janet gently suggested that she should see her therapist and was promptly mocked for having one. By their second week together Janet had retreated to the couch and discovered that sleeping there was almost impossible. Janet spent days hovering around the bedroom door as Cindy lay in bed with Esther watching television. On the night Cindy sullenly announced that she had decided to have lunch with Andrew, Janet snuck in the bathroom with the phone and made an appointment with the locksmith.

Janet claimed, "And I'm not interested in digging up any more ghosts from my past." James was unaware of how aggressive he sounded, "Can't you do it for me?" "What…" She wanted to change the subject, "Does that arouse you?" "No," James stammered, "I mean yes of course it does but that's not why I want you to tell me about her." She looked perplexed, "But why then?" He drained his glass before saying, "I'd just like to get to know you better." "Because," Janet coyly deduced, "you want to sleep with both of us." The words caught in his throat, "Could you arrange something like that?" Janet said, "why you dirty boy," as Esther entered the living room, "oh look," with her bushy tail raised like a swaying periscope, "who decided to crash our little party," and as the cat walked over to the couch she added, "speaking of threesomes… this kitty just loves them… come here sweetheart." Esther cautiously smelled the laces on both of his sneakers before leaping onto the cushion between them. Janet ran her right hand through Esther's thick fur, "I'm afraid that you haven't been making yourself very clear," and then caressed her chin with the tips of her fingernails, "how unusual for such a gifted and ambitious writer." Esther began to purr. James looked down at the scuffed tips of his sneakers, "When were you going to tell me that she called?" "That really isn't any of your business." James repeated the question as a demand, "When were you going to tell me that," that cast a shadow over her bewildered expression, "that you're planning on seeing her again?" Hunching her shoulders, "I just told you that I'm not interested in digging up any more ghosts from my past."

Fourth Thursday in July

S tephanie picked the phone up before the second ring, "hello," hoping that Alan was finally confirming for tonight, "oh hi mom." She studied the overcast sky and considered returning to the apartment to get an umbrella. A Manhattan bound F train pulled up to the platform as she descended the stairs. "Okay," the alarm clock on the night stand, "actually I was," indicated that it was one o'clock, "on my way out the door," therefore it was ten in California where her mother was calling from, "I really don't have much time." The clouds gradually revealed patches of blue sky. A crowd stood before the open doors while the people exiting the train shouldered their way past. Her mother had recently moved from Philadelphia to San Diego, where her third husband owned a camera store. The three young Indian boys from the first floor were gathered around an overturned mountain bike. She entered the air-conditioned train just before the doors closed. Stephanie had met her second stepfather only once, at their wedding in '98, and always had trouble remembering his name. They looked up from the detached chain and waved hello with grease-smeared palms. "I'm taking the day off," Stephanie cleared her throat, "I'm not feeling very well," and ended her sentence with a sigh. She crossed the street before Vincent's Hair Design and then walked towards the corner. "No," she pulled away the sheet, "it's not that," swung her bare legs off the bed, "I'm probably getting my period," and stood on the hardwood floor, "but I have an appointment in Manhattan that I can't be late for." The Chinese man from the liquor store was leaning on a parking meter with a blank expression on his face. The conductor announced the next station stop before the train pulled away from the platform. Holding the phone away from her ear, "well," away from the laughter on the line, "I'm glad that amuses you," as she crossed the bedroom. Women in flowing saris were pushing baby strollers down

37th Avenue. A Hispanic man reading the *Daily News* was dressed in a navy blue security uniform. **DEADLY DRIVING LESSON** "Why would you call me during the day," she opened the closet and yanked a black skirt off a hanger, "if you thought I was at work?" The gray cat from the newsstand ducked between the wheels of a parked car. "Isn't it a little early in the day for you to be doing this?" Stephanie's passing reflection in the furniture store window was superimposed upon a living room set. **Brooklyn Man Dies, Teen Critical As Minivan Jumps Barriers Into Water** "No I'm not," she examined herself in the mirror above the dresser, "I'm not attacking you," in lacy black panties and a snug pink T-shirt that outlined her yellow bra, "But when did you start drinking again?" The grainy black and white photograph of a minivan being pulled out of New York Bay. A blue haired retiree in a lime green polyester pantsuit weighed a half-pound of cherries outside the Korean grocery. She overheard the voices on her mother's television while they shared an awkward pause. **Madonna Rocks The Garden On Her Drowned World/ Substitute For Love Tour** A blind man and the woman clutching his arm were talking about where they were going for lunch while waiting for the light to change. The black and white photograph of Madonna in a plaid mini-skirt and a tight top adorned with thin patent leather straps. "Does everything," Stephanie turned away from the mirror, "have to be a test with you?" She walked by the table displaying battery operated plastic toys and their cacophony of canned rhythms, sirens and whistles. She pulled the skirt up to her waist, "What am I supposed to say?" Indian women and their children stood outside the grocery store on 74th street, where Stephanie bought henna for her hair, as the smell of fresh basil mingled with tamarind and curry powder hung in the humid air. "Fine…" her blue heels were in the closet, "I've been just fine." The sun emerged from behind the clouds and cast diffused shadows on the sidewalk. She stepped into the shoes, "I'd really like to visit," and leaned over to buckle the thin ankle straps, "you know that," around her narrow ankles, "but I am so busy at work." **Woman Hit With Brick, Man Busted** The smell of cooking oil and rotting vegetables mingled with car exhaust. The table displaying gilded passages from the Koran and framed color photographs of pilgrims in white robes kneeling towards Mecca. **Bronx Girl Was Killed By Cousin—Boy Admits Shooting** She walked out of the bedroom, "it's fine," with the telephone tucked beneath her ear. A shop window displaying gold filigree jewelry made her think of the earrings she had bought several months ago, the ones with tiny flowers woven to the tails of songbirds, that she rarely wore. A colorful poster of Ganesha, the boy God with the elephant's head, was taped to a glass door. The F train swept through the 65th street station and the crowds waiting on the local watched it pass.

Stephanie really missed Alan; it had been a week since they had seen each other and then it had only been for dinner. They had watched the sun set while sitting at a candlelit table at The River Café drinking Gewürztramminer. She had asked him about the two weeks he spent with his wife and daughter in Martha's Vineyard and he described it in a few laconic sentences. "You never talk about your wife," Stephanie had quietly mused. He leaned back in the chair, "I can't imagine that she is of any interest to you." "You're right," she laughed, "she isn't." He smiled, "Then why did you say that?" She raised her glass in a toast, "I was paying you a compliment."

Stephanie retrieved her purse from the kitchen table, "I spoke to dad last week and he sounded fine." She was offered a seat as the train pulled out of the 21ˢᵗ Street/Queensbridge Station. "Listen, mom, I'll call you later but I really have to go," she pressed the end button on the phone after adding a curt, "goodbye." The young man sitting beside her was engrossed in a guide to writing fiction.

Elements of Plot in a Narrative

Alan and Stephanie rarely spoke on the phone and infrequently exchanged emails, yet she often found herself obsessing over him. There were times when it felt like she was falling in love with him.

The plot in a dramatic or narrative work is constituted by its events and actions, as these are rendered and ordered towards achieving particular artistic and emotional effects.

Or could easily fall in love with him, she knew better of course, and it was only when the distance between them stretched out for weeks and grew insurmountable that it felt like she could be falling in love.

1. Initial Situation—The Beginning. It is always the first incident that makes a story move.

Stephanie hadn't been involved with anyone since her fiancé abruptly ended their five-year relationship the year prior, claiming that he needed to be closer to his family, and moved back to London. She had learned on Christmas day that he was living with another woman, since then she had convinced herself that she would never find anyone with whom she was so compatible and reluctantly endured being alone although it was often very painful.

2. Conflict or Problem— A goal the main character of the story has to achieve.

Her relationship with Alan often made her happy and it gave her a confidence that she never knew she possessed.

3. Complications—Obstacles the main character has to overcome.

Alan paid her rent, covered her bills, bought her beautiful shoes and lingerie, took her to expensive restaurants and had promised to get her a high paying job. He made no unreasonable demands on her and the sex was usually satisfying, provided he was sober. She was treated like an equal—not like property—or as Karen recently claimed that she had become the occasional plaything of a wealthy alcoholic.

4. Climax—Highest point of interest in the story.

And so what if their relationship wasn't going to last? He had made it clear to her from the very beginning that they had to keep things casual and had even encouraged her to date other men.

5. Suspense—Point of tension. It arouses the interest of the readers.

Love doesn't last either. She now understood that her marriage, assuming it would have happened, would not have survived. Her ex-fiancé couldn't face conflicts or challenges, he always fled them, and his cowardice invariably followed.

6. Denouement or Resolution—What happens to the character after overcoming all the obstacles/failing to achieve the desired result and reaching/not reaching his or her goals.

In retrospect her failed engagement was nothing more than a useful life experience. For Stephanie the time she spent with Alan, however infrequent it may be, was it's own reward.

7. Conclusion—The end of the story.

She removed a quarter from her wallet while walking up the stairs at the West 4th Street station. The crowds gathered around the high chain-link fence were watching the basketball games. She dropped the quarter in the payphone slot while clutching the warm receiver in her left hand and dialed his office number from memory. Cabs sped along 6th Avenue or slowed to abrupt stops to drop off and pick up fares. She asked Alan's secretary if he was available and then gave her name. Stephanie stated, "I am becoming my mother," after he said hello. His warm laughter caused her to smile, "Would you ever call your mother," as she imagined him standing in his office with his sleeves rolled up to his elbows, "and apologize for being a bad liar?" A group of teenagers ogled her breasts as they sauntered by. "You know," Alan closed the door to his office, "I think I have done that," and sat on the edge of his desk. She turned away from the crowds and faced the silver keypad on the payphone, "How did you do it?" He glanced at the digital desk clock, "I'll tell you later," and watched a few seconds pass. She swallowed hard before asking, "Tonight?" Alan sighed wistfully, "I'm afraid I can't tonight... I have meetings until seven and dinner with a group of potential investors who just might be up for backing some choice property in Williamsburg," before half-jokingly suggesting that she could drop by later in the afternoon for a quick fuck on his desk. "Sure," while rolling her eyes, "but what would your secretary say?" Paying no attention to his giddy explanation and simply waiting for him to pause long enough to change the subject. They talked about their upcoming weekend together in East Hampton. He described the house overlooking the bay where they were going to stay as modest and added, "that it's just far enough away from everything else." When her quarter ran out she had enough time to tell him that she really missed him before the call was terminated.

Exclusions Apply—Part 3

The wooden blinds drawn before the amber streetlight outside her bedroom window, "The last memory," projected a thin row of horizontal shadows across the bed, "of seeing my father alive," onto the wall behind them, "was when I was sitting on the edge of his bed watching Nadia Comaneci," and a portion of the ceiling, "on the parallel bars during the summer Olympics." They were lying naked beneath a thick down comforter with their arms and legs entwined. Earlier, Janet had been able to appease James with earnest reassurances that his insecurities about any potential infidelities were unfounded and finally convince him that she had no interest in renewing her relationship with Cindy by describing how rapidly that affair had disintegrated. He cleared his throat before asking, "What summer was this?" The resolve in her tone while relating this memory, "the summer of," countered her mounting suspicions, "July of Seventy-Six," that the events she had been prompted to relate would be coolly deconstructed and fictionalized in his yet to be written first novel. "That was four years before I was born." The warmth in her tone, "well," and the bottle of champagne they had shared while sitting on the couch, "I was seventeen that summer," fused with the clarity drawn from their intimacy, "and this city was another world then," had led to his repeated proclamations of love. A pair of headlights slowly crossed the ceiling while he waited for her to continue speaking. Janet looked out the window as the cab she was sitting in sped across the Brooklyn Bridge. "I knew that…" she began again in a dry whisper, "I knew that something was wrong," and the skyscrapers in mid-town were brown silhouettes in the smog filled distance. He caressed the nape of her neck, "How so?" The humid air blowing through the wide-open rear windows smelled of tar and diesel fumes. "He was really out of it after his last operation," she cleared her throat, "and was having trouble walking," while recalling the emptiness that had filled her chest, "and I was really reluctant," as the cab gradually descended the ramp leading to the northbound lanes of the FDR drive. Cupping his palms over her breasts, "Where was this?" A car horn was muffled by the closed windows and then silence ensued as she placed her chin on his shoulder and closed her eyes, "in Turtle Bay." "Where is that?" A tug pushing a gray barge filled with garbage down the East River moved slowly against the incoming tide while a large flock of seagulls trailed above it. "It's the neighborhood by the U.N." The sun broke through a gap in the clouds as a passenger helicopter took off from the roof of the Pan-Am building. "That's where I grew up." The cab driver had asked if she'd been following the news about that busload of children that had been kidnapped in Northern California. "Why is it called that?" Janet shook her head before saying that she had only read the headlines and that it sounded really terrible. "There was once a creek there and the Dutch had a turtle farm… I think they make silly pets." The driver nodded before activating the blinker and merging into the exit lane. "Why is that?" Janet removed the cigarettes from her purse and tapped one out of the pack while claiming that she had enough to worry about and then placed it between her lips with trembling fingers. "You can't cuddle with a turtle." The driver watched her in the rearview mirror, as she finally lit the cigarette with a small green disposable lighter, before asking if she was okay. "Not like cats at least," James kissed her on the forehead before asking, "Where's Esther?" She exhaled a thin cloud of smoke before saying that she wasn't sure and then looked away from the reflection of his watery blue eyes as the cab slowly pulled through the intersection. "She is probably sleeping on the couch." The Saturday afternoon traffic was sparse and they arrived in front of the apartment building before Janet had smoked half of the cigarette. "I've never eaten turtle before." She paid the driver and thanked him for his concern while getting out of the cab. "I hear they taste just like chicken." She stood on the sidewalk and finished her cigarette. "Why were you reluctant?" The marble lobby, "I had a premonition," was as cold as a walk-in refrigerator. "I really can't imagine what New York was like then." She chewed on her lower lip while waiting for the elevator as the gooseflesh rose on her forearms. "It was a good time to be young." The doorman behind the desk glanced up from his comic book and nodded hello. "Do you ever feel guilty about being reluctant?" When the elevator finally arrived, "At times I do," she stepped into it, "although we were never very close," and pressed ten before taking the black plastic band out of the front pocket of her blue jeans. The ceiling fan circulated stale air in the narrow mirrored mahogany space. "Why is that?" She ran her fingers through her long brown hair, "My father had always been unavailable," pulled it back into a pony tail, "even when I was very young," then tied it back with the elastic band. "Do you want to fuck again," when the elevator stopped on ten she considered taking it back to the lobby as the doors slowly opened, "Or do you want to talk?" Her silent footfalls, "Do you not want to do this anymore," moved slowly along the carpeted hallway. She removed the keys from her purse, "I never talk," and unlocked the door, "about this anymore." Turning the cold knob in her right hand. "So he was alone after the surgery?" She entered the apartment, "He had fired his nurse," and soon discovered the wide blood stain, "the day before he did it," on the damp beige carpet, "and that was the day before I found him," in front of the bathroom door, "when the neighbors downstairs called me at my aunt's in Brooklyn Heights." She pushed open the door and stood there. "You know that we don't have to talk about this if you don't want to." Janet recalled the memories that followed, "my father had been in a lot of pain," and arranged them in sequence once more, "and he had been very depressed about their separation," like playing a familiar hand of worn cards. She walked to the phone in the living room and called the police. "Where was your mother?" The conversation with the female dispatcher, "in Rome with her new boyfriend," who kept her on the line until the two police officers arrived, "the way people couldn't look at me then…"and they just stood there with their backs to the bookshelves and asked a lot of aggressive questions, "like at the wake when my father's partners talked about how honest he was," until the ambulance finally arrived. "Had they heard anything?" The coroner got there an hour later. "Who?" They removed her father from the tub and placed him in a black body bag. "The downstairs neighbors." And when they finally wheeled it out of the bathroom on a gurney, "He slit his wrists in the bathtub," she fainted, "there wasn't anything to hear." "What did you do?" She came to on the couch, "I called the police," and discovered her aunt standing above her sobbing uncontrollably, "and then I really don't remember what happened next." The wind was pressing on the windows as it pushed through the bare trees. She opened her eyes, "I think I've blocked it out," removed her head from his shoulder, "well," and quietly sighed, "now you know." James looked closely at her face, "you said that the neighbors called you," in the faint amber light, "that's why I asked if they might have heard something." Janet blinked twice, "they were very close to my parents." He nodded, "so that's why." She turned over on her back, "they used to play bridge together every Wednesday night," and rested her head on a pillow, "and when he didn't answer the door they got concerned." "Did your mother remarry?" She nodded, "twice," with a smile in her voice.

First Saturday in August

"You know, there's going to be a full moon tonight." The pines surrounding the deck were spotted with lichen. "Can we go for a walk later and take a look at it?" Massive cumulus clouds with pink underbellies had crowded above the bay. "Alright," the drone of cicadas, "we'll get a better view from the ocean side," and intermittent notes from songbirds flitting among the trees accompanied the view, "But haven't you had enough beach for one day?" The wooden deck gave off the warm smell of creosote. "No," two wine glasses filled with rosé, "not at all," were on the wide railing, "and a moon tan will soothe my burn," beside the bottle of Tavel nestled in a copper ice bucket. Alan had dutifully coated Stephanie's shoulders and dabbed her nose with a torn aloe leaf after they showered together. "Does it feel any better?" They were on their first bottle of wine. "I feel so relaxed, but I'm sure that you're getting tired of hearing that." Nearly invisible flames wavered above the graying charcoal briquettes as fat sizzled off the blackened grill. Alan turned to her, "on the contrary." A CD of Coltrane's ballads that she had discovered in the living room was playing on the stereo. "That is such a sweet thing to say." The sliding screen door was dotted with ladybugs. He stood before the wooden cutting board, "well," grinding peppercorns onto a pair of plump duck breasts, "it's true." The potato salad she'd prepared with olive oil, dry vermouth, chopped scallions and a pinch of sea salt was in the earthenware bowl on the table. "Could you imagine us together out here all year round?" Thick slices of garden tomatoes sprinkled with olive oil and garnished with basil leaves were arranged on the wide glass platter next to the bowl of potato salad. "It isn't going to get any better than this." Four folding canvas chairs were situated around the wooden picnic table. She was wearing a yellow bikini top and cut-off jeans, "How can you be so sure that it isn't going to get any better than this?" The short flight of wooden stairs that lead to the bay sank into the yellow sand. "I think I would go crazy out here in a few weeks." Her damp hair was pulled back in a ponytail, "How can you say such a thing?" An elderly couple stood by the shore and watched their Collie retrieve a tennis ball from a set of knee-high breakers. "That always happens when I go for too long without working." She wrapped her arms around his waist and held him close, "I'll help you get over that," then kissed him on the ear, "and keep you from going crazy." The broad bay with its glassy rose-hued surface swayed beneath the clouds. He was wearing khaki shorts, "I think that women have a much easier time not working" and a white Polo shirt. A few gulls circled overhead. "How so?" Three people on the deck of a sailboat, fifty yards from the shore, prepared to launch it. "In the roles they're expected to perform," he pulled away from her, "that job you had when we first met wasn't the least bit important to you and it certainly didn't last very long." "Are you referring to all women," she placed her hands on her hips, "or just the ones you're attracted to?" He turned to her and nodded, "all of them." A cloud slowly passed before the sun. She shook her head dismissively, "I really hate your stereotypes." He regarded her child-like indignation, "but you're okay with having me pay your rent," while weighing her rapidly diminishing charms. "You know that," she countered, "I would rather be working at something that makes a difference." She had begun to put a serious strain on his energies, "Really?" and the time she demanded from him was becoming increasingly counterproductive, "like what for instance?" "I mean, doing something, having a job, something that I care about," she shook her head, " but I really don't think you want me to get a job," and was surprised by how quickly their conversation had turned into another argument, "talk about stereotypes," before recalling the fifth of Stoli that had materialized on the kitchen counter while she was slicing the tomatoes. He turned away from her, "I've had to do quite a bit of finagling on your behalf," and attended to the smoking coals, "and that took up a lot more time then I had initially anticipated." "Like what… What sort of finagling?" "What difference does it make now that you've gotten your interview," he waved the tongs over the flames, "which is merely a formality." She made an effort to appease him, "Why won't you tell me what you did that got me the job then?" "You do things for people, and in turn, they do things for you, like lending you their beach house for the weekend. And don't forget that when you ask someone for a favor you *are* expected to reciprocate." She attempted to disarm him, "So what have I done to deserve all of this?" And when that failed she claimed, "my wanting you to help me get a job isn't a betrayal of our relationship." "Wanting to make a difference…Is that what you just said?" He drained his glass and chuckled, "Would it be possible for you to be any more vague than that?" A warm breeze forced its way through the pines. "I said that I wanted a job that I enjoyed. Why are you in such a bad mood?" "Like I just told you," he took the bottle from the ice bucket, "that interview on Monday is merely a formality," and spilled some wine while refilling his glass, "so shouldn't you be out shopping for a new wardrobe," then pointed, "you'd been out of work for a few months before we met." She shrugged before quietly saying, "about three months." He set the bottle in the ice bucket, "And you were okay with that?" "Not really… I was broke… I mean my father helped me out a lot but not having any money or health insurance really sucks… you should try it some time. " "But you weren't really looking for a job?" She exhaled slowly through her nose, "I've always had a very hard time with rejection." He knew the answer before asking, "Did you go on any interviews?" She shrugged again, "I must have gone on one or two." He tried to sound insulted, "And you just couldn't find the right job?" "At least one interview, obviously," she decided that tonight wouldn't be a good time to tell him that her period was almost a month late. "You went on one interview and that was when," he jutted out his chin, "you had no other choice but to get a job?" She had wanted to tell him over the weekend, "I was broke and I couldn't borrow any more money," so they could discuss their options, "and I took the first job that came along." "I'm certain that you could have found a better job if you had bothered to look." "But then," she protested, "we would have never met." He didn't respond. She resolved to take the test at home, and if the results were positive, confront him over the phone, what was the point of creating another conflict? He regarded the dark pink wine in his glass. She crossed her arms beneath her breasts, "and that makes what you said before sound so disingenuous." "Oh, does it?" He swirled the wine while adding, "men are forced into a very narrow set of roles," then held the rim of the glass beneath his nose and sniffed it, "that are pounded into our impressionable heads at a very young age," before taking a sip, "roles that have to be followed to the letter in order to insure our success as individuals… whereas with women it is much easier for them to live comfortably on the margins because less has always been expected of them." "That's bullshit and besides not all men are like you." "No it isn't bullshit Stephanie, to have ambition and talent isn't bullshit… and men who've perfected those roles as children… they succeed." She rolled her eyes, "you're just talking about yourself." It was his turn to shrug, "of course I am." She conceded his point to avoid another argument, "I know that you're very hard working and ambitious," while eyeing the wine glass in his right hand, "but maybe money doesn't mean all that much to me," before looking down at the narrow wooden slats between their bare feet, "my family didn't have a lot of money… we weren't poor—" "You're from a suburban middle class family." She nodded, "and after my parent's split we had even less." "You went to public schools," he counted the points off on his free hand, "you haven't finished college, yet, and you've never even been to Europe… But so what?" A broad ray of sunlight fell on the full sails of the boat as it glided toward the center of the bay. "Maybe I'd be happy just being a secretary and riding the subway to work five days a week." The sailboat gradually shrank into a silhouette before the opposing shore. "There would be nothing wrong with that, assuming it paid well enough," he assured her, "and nobody would ever expect anything more from you." "Except you, because you place way too much importance on money." "You say that now but you're always pestering me to help you." "Because I don't want to be dependent on anyone." "Do you know how much a weekend in this house is worth," he sipped his wine, "in August?" "No I don't," she shook her head, "and it doesn't matter to me anyway." He wet his lips and grinned, "But I am just anyone?" The cloud had drifted away from the sun. "Sometimes you make me very happy." He took a step forward, "Just sometimes?" She squinted from the glare off the bay, "when you make an effort. You make me very happy."

Intermission

When Janet pressed her palms together, "besides," and clasped her hands, "my bed is much larger than yours," the lights in the restaurant were dimmed a notch. "How would you know that?" James asked. She smiled with palpable anticipation, "I think it's a safe assumption," while assessing his appearance, "and wouldn't it be more interesting," as if for the first time, "for you to find out for yourself," when looking up from the remaindered copy of *The Satyricon* in her hands and acknowledging his attention with a discreet nod, "Mr. Intrusive?" He swallowed hard, "let's leave at intermission," before mirroring her appraisal with a warm smile.

They stood next to each other on the crowded sidewalk as he looked down the street for an approaching cab. James had commented on how beautiful the evening was as the stoplight above the intersection changed from red to green. Janet stated that her lamb was much better than Eric Asimov claimed it would be. Three cabs sped past his outstretched arm as she added that her potatoes had been perfectly seasoned and that she shouldn't have eaten all of them. A cab finally pulled up to the curb and he opened the rear door for her.

She nudged his ankle with the tip of her pointed shoe, "you know, I really liked that story you gave me." Furrowing his brow, "You don't think it's too melodramatic?" "No," shaking her head, "not at all," without taking her eyes off his mouth, "it's quite sad and really advanced for someone your age." He delivered the next line with the confident ease, "you're only saying that because you like me," that had evolved out of their rehearsals. "Well that, and because you are so *profoundly* objective," she ended her line with an exasperated sigh. "You think so?" When she suggested, "but you might have that backwards," the striking hostess seated an elderly couple at the table beside them.

Janet told him that she was very happy they were able to have such a pleasant dinner together and added that the wine the waiter had recommended was perfect although they should have ordered a bottle instead of allowing him to refill their glasses whenever he walked by. James nodded in agreement as another block passed by in a blur of neon and glowing florescent storefronts.

"My story isn't too episodic?" She wanted to tease him about the questions he pressed on her after she offered him generous interpretations of his fiction, "you're quite fond of that word," but didn't want to risk hurting his feelings. He jerked forward in the metal seat that creaked beneath him, "What do you mean?" At times the coddled boy seated before her seemed so hopelessly young, "that's the third time you used it tonight."

The driver made a left onto Houston.

He frowned, "I'm being serious." She regarded his expression with half-hearted concern, "I'm just kidding," then realized that when she was his age this self-obsessive task he had fretfully tied himself to would have been dismissed as absurd. He clutched the napkin in his clammy fists, "Well is it or not?" "Isn't fiction episodic by definition?" He shook his head, "you know what I mean." She wanted to encourage him to inch further away from this all-encompassing and profoundly claustrophobic task, "Do I?" "Come on," looking closely at her eyes, "I'm being serious." She conceded his question with a shrug, "the story could be read as sensational because the event was," while the small flame burning faintly in the frosted glass candleholder wavered in a draft.

He thanked her for dinner and then kissed her on the cheek as the cab swerved into the center lane. She told him that her ex always made a huge production out of going to expensive restaurants, that he had the ability to ruin every meal with his petty demands on unlucky waiters and how his obnoxious behavior inevitably summoned the attention of a soon to be flustered maitre d' whose own hand-wringing attempts at placating that jackass of a man meant that every meal they had together became an excruciating exercise in humiliation.

The waiter crossed in front of the audience on cue and presented her with the bill. James slowly reached for it, "I've got it." She took the wallet out of her black purse, "don't be silly," that had been hanging over the metal chair, "remember this was my idea." He leaned back in the chair, "How much is it?" She examined the bill, "it's a bit pricey considering the quality of the ingredients," in her right hand and then muttered, "but don't worry about that," without looking up from the narrow columns of handwritten numbers.

She continued damning her ex, who had just married some Long Island whore, with a scathing description of his shortcomings in bed. James asked for more details and Janet promptly listed the number of ways she had been accommodating and then described how quickly their sex became routine. He squeezed her hand while asking if they ever watched porn together. Janet said that she found pornography to be unimaginative as three fire trucks with sirens blaring raced past. She quietly asked if he liked to smoke marijuana as the cab came to a slow stop. James shook his head while claiming that it made him really paranoid. She mentioned that she had some really good pot stashed away in her freezer and perhaps if they smoked it together he would have a better time.

He began to blush, "I'll pay for the play," as a sheepish grin covered his face.

She dutifully closed her eyes just before he kissed her on the mouth. Headlights briefly filled the cab's interior as they clutched each other in the backseat.

"And the wine was…" she looked at him closely, "How many glasses did you have?"

She removed the silver compact from her purse and inspected her mouth as he reassured her that she was very beautiful and that he was very lucky—extraordinarily lucky in fact—to be this close to her. She thanked him while slipping the compact back into her purse.

"I had as many glasses as you did," he rubbed his nose with the back of his right hand before adding, "it was very good wine." She placed her gold American Express card beneath the bill, "it was twelve dollars a glass."

The driver lay on his horn as they sped through a long yellow light.

"Usually I don't drink wine," he drummed his fingers on the table, "but that was great," then looked around the dining room before asking, "Why would he give you the bill anyway?"

James slipped a ten through the slat in the bulletproof partition and told the driver to keep the change.

He frowned, "Don't you think that's rude?" "No, not really," Janet wondered how he would thank her for dinner, "I was the one who asked for it."

James stood between two parked cars and admired her stockinged legs as she slid out of the cab. He reached into the breast pocket of his dinner jacket to reassure himself that the short story was still there. They held hands while walking toward the cluster of people by the door who were stepping on their cigarettes and removing money from their wallets.

She pursed her lips, "it may be a French restaurant but we're not in France."

A large black and white photograph of Rainer Werner Fassbinder wearing aviator sunglasses and brandishing a pistol had been taped to the gallery window.

He nodded, "I guess we should—" As she interjected, "—Are you still…"

Copies of the October issue of the *Brooklyn Rail* were stacked on the floor by the door and the Kim Jones drawing on the cover caught Janet's eye.

"I'm sorry, what were you going to say?"

He paid their admission and then they found a pair of chairs in the center of the gallery.

"No, you go ahead."

The lights faded to black and in the darkness the actors got up, crossed to the sliding door leading to the gallery office and disappeared behind it.

I stood up when the house lights came on and walked toward the door. When Cindy turned around, alarmed that I had left so quickly, she noticed Janet sitting two rows behind her. The audience looked engaged and I realized that the actors had gotten the scene across. Cindy quickly turned around as Janet smiled in surprise. A live version of Roxy Music's "If There is Something" followed me onto the sidewalk. Cindy faced the two empty metal chairs as a rush of contradicting emotions threatened to overwhelm her; in just a few weeks she had hollowed out what human elements Janet possessed and her superficial façade had been honed into an angular caricature that was tormented by an insatiable loneliness as she suffered the disastrous results of her impulsive judgments. I lit a cigarette while walking to the bodega on the corner. Cindy didn't know how to respond to what she hoped would be a compliment, but how could the scene possibly be interpreted as a passionate testament to the enduring power of their relationship? The sidewalk beneath the streetlight glistened in a broad pool of pale light and my silhouette was cast upon the windows of the parked cars. Or would the pain and anger over Janet's betrayal steep this bizarre coincidence in cynicism? The radio behind the counter at the bodega was tuned to the World Series and Boston was up by two in the bottom of the third. The sound of Janet's voice filled her head as a familiar hand rested on her shoulder, "I had no idea that you were so talented," she was standing above Cindy with a bright smile on her painted face,

"And how have you been?" A large black and white cat ran down the bodega aisle as I walked toward the refrigerator. Cindy stood up, "I can't believe that you're here," and when Janet kissed her on the cheek she managed to whisper, "what a surprise," as they embraced. I slid open the glass door and removed a tall cold can of Ballantine. Cindy opened her eyes and noticed the young man standing beside Janet in a thrift store suit, "Hello, I'm James," as he extended his right hand. The man behind the counter placed the beer in a brown paper bag and I slid it into the front left pocket of my black corduroy jacket.

Third Saturday in August

S tephanie sat on the edge of the bathtub with the phone in her left hand and waited for a wave of nausea to subside. The empty blue and white box was on the edge of the tub, the unfolded illustrated instructions lay on the tiles by her bare feet and water from the bathroom faucet was dripping on the narrow plastic stick in the bottom of the sink. The dark blue cross that appeared almost immediately in the tiny indicator box signified her positive results and relieved almost as many fears as it created. Her ears were ringing as she bounced her knees up and down while drawing deep breaths through her nose. The smell of the new shower curtain mingled with the lavender scent of hair conditioner. She hadn't been this aware of her body since breaking her collarbone when she was seventeen. Her then boyfriend's Honda Civic had been sideswiped by a pickup and in slow motion the car careened off the road and rolled twice before plowing into the trunk of an oak. After they had been pried away from the shattered windshield and haze of smoking engine fluids, one of the EMS attendants informed her that their seatbelts had saved their lives. The shock of the crash and the throbbing pain in her chest was tempered by the wonderment of being alive.

A toilet flushed upstairs and that was followed by the sound of someone taking a shower. Her nausea gradually subsided as she stared at her unpainted toenails on the beige floor tiles.

Alan had given her a check for three thousand dollars the same night the condom broke. He had been too drunk to realize that it had shredded around his erection; their orgasms had been nearly simultaneous. As she rinsed herself out in the tub, he stood in the bathroom doorway and assured her that it had taken his wife at least six months to get pregnant. After drying herself with a blue bath towel they returned to her candle-lit bedroom. Alan gradually dispelled her anxiety by assuring her that he would never leave her.

The realization that his wife's difficulty to conceive had nothing to do with him accompanied another wave of nausea.

Last night Stephanie had considered calling her mother to tell her that she was probably pregnant. While lecturing Stephanie about the importance of always practicing safe sex her mother never failed to mention having to get an abortion when she was in high school. The idea of telling her mother that she had to get an abortion was crushed by the depressing realization that she was becoming just like her; the long string of failed relationships and her emotional dependence on deeply self-destructive and emotionally detached men, dropping out of college after her sophomore year, her excessive drinking—especially over this summer and her inability to hold down a steady job all mirrored her mother.

Thinking of the cold cans of ginger ale in the refrigerator and the half-eaten roll of Tums on the dresser calmed her stomach.

She took a deep breath and exhaled while dialing Karen's number. She imagined Karen grappling with the ringing phone just before she answered. "It's positive," Stephanie cleared her throat, "I'm sorry did you have a late night?" She pressed her knees together while listening to Karen's groggy response. The resolve in Stephanie's tone, "I am going to call Planned Parenthood after I get off the phone with you," underscored her terse conviction.

Weeks ago Stephanie and Alan had spent an idyllic Saturday at the beach and that night he launched into her without the slightest provocation. Alan had drunkenly picked her apart with an entire catalogue of her meticulously collected faults. She finally called him on his abusive behavior on Sunday morning while they were having brunch at The Laundry. Alan simply claimed that she was needy and hypersensitive. She went for a long walk along the shore afterwards, as the bay turned the same shade of gray as the sky, and concluded that their relationship was finished.

"Yeah but I'm not his victim," Stephanie tugged at her lower lip with her thumb and forefinger, "this just *happened,* you know."

She returned from her walk just in time to overhear him placating his wife over the phone. Alan berated Stephanie for wandering off alone and claimed that she couldn't possibly appreciate all of the things he had done for her. The three-hour drive back to the city in the pouring rain was spent in sullen silence—broken only by his furious outburst at other drivers. He left her in front of her building and drove off without a word.

"Besides, he already thinks that I'm incompetent. What would he say now if he knew that I was pregnant?" Stephanie swallowed the sour taste in her mouth, "And if it isn't over already it will be as soon as I tell him… I'm really sorry… so please don't be mad at me for doing this," she stood up, "it's not just because I don't have anyone else to talk to," and walked out of the bathroom with the phone tucked beneath her left ear. "No," she crossed to the bedroom, "no I don't need any money," took the Tums off the dresser, "it works on a sliding scale there," and peeled three from the roll. She put two of them in her mouth, "I think it's about eight-thirty," and began chewing on the chalky tablets, "you know, if this was a weekday I would already be at work," while rolling the third one between her fingers. "It's like forty thousand a year before taxes," she glanced at the travel alarm clock on the night stand, "yeah, it's a real job and I'm really happy there which is pretty strange when you think about how I got it," it was ten past eight. She sat on the edge of the unmade bed with her back to the open window, "no the results were almost immediate. I mean I peed onto the stick and by the time I washed my hands there was the blue cross." A plane flew above her building. "Do you want to call me before you leave?" She smiled at the thought of Karen's company. "I mean I'll be around all day." Sunlight reflecting off the windows of the apartment building across the street, "okay, okay… maybe some chicken soup," cast a bright triangle of silver light onto her bedroom wall. "Okay," Stephanie said, "so I'll see you around noon," before pressing the end button on the phone.

Four More Years

I woke up on the carpet as the radio repeated the election results that I had attempted to erase with a bottle of wine and a six-pack. At five a.m. the Republican pundits on the radio, Giuliani in particular, were demanding that Kerry concede. I swallowed a few aspirin with a glass of water, turned out the lights and crawled beneath the covers. The streetlight in front of my bedroom window went out just before I fell asleep.

My cell phone was vibrating on the floor beside the bed as it rang. I picked it up and pressed talk before Cindy said, "Hey Donald, how's it going?" I squinted at the sun that was suspended in the tall bedroom window, "not good at all." She was standing in front of a shuttered storefront church, "Did I wake you up?" "What time is it?" I rasped. A young black woman pushing a stroller walked past her, "almost noon."

Bands of windswept clouds expanded in the pale sky. "My head is killing me." A plane bound for Laguardia flew overhead. "Are you doing anything today?" I rested my head on the pillows and closed my eyes, "I'm not even going to try." "So you're at home," She sounded so happy, "at the new place on Spencer Court?" The co-pilot instructed the passengers to fasten their seatbelts as the plane descended through the patchy clouds. "Yeah why?" The oak tree down the block, "I'm on the corner of DeKalb and Bedford," swayed in the wind, "and I really need to see you," while shedding its brown leaves. The view from the cockpit revealed a low lying grid-work of houses, factory chimneys, and incinerators that were spewing pale smoke, slow moving traffic filled the bridges spanning the East River and the broad expressways. "You're there right now?" The plane flew above elevated subway lines as trains moved between the stations. "I've got to talk to you." A runway bordered by blinking red lights approached in the rapidly diminishing distance. "You're on the corner right now?" "Yeah that's what I just said." I opened my eyes, "What's the matter?" She began walking toward my building, "I'll tell you in a minute," and crushed a few acorns beneath her thick heels, "It's number ten right?" A half-dozen tall cans of Ballantine were on the carpet where I had passed out. "Give me a minute though." "Why," she stopped walking, "what's the matter?" A heavy bass rhythm was vibrating the car pulling up to the corner. "Can you pick me up a cup of coffee," I noticed the stains on my T-shirt, "milk no sugar, please," and that I wasn't wearing any pants. The tinted window on the driver's side opened as animated rap was punctuated with loud gunshots. "Yeah sure," Cindy added, "I'll be there in a few minutes," before hanging up.

They got high while sitting together on Janet's couch, "Remember that woman," with Esther nestled on Cindy's lap and purring quietly beneath her caresses, "that I was telling you about?" "The one who was at the play on Friday?" Janet's small brass bowl was in Cindy's left hand, "yes that one," and smoking from both ends. "The one who left before the second act?" Janet tactfully apologized for hurting Cindy before wondering out-loud if what she had recently endured had been a suitable lesson in humility, but thankfully because of this happy coincidence, and then Janet's voice trailed off because words weren't really necessary to complete the sentence they were now sharing on her couch. "The woman that the character was based on." The cup of hot coffee warmed my left hand, "What about her?" Cindy dutifully accepted Janet's apology and even shared some of the blame for what had happened last April. "I spent the night at her place," Janet kissed Cindy on the mouth and then they embraced, "and I told Andrew last night," her eyes were shining in the sunlight flooding the windows behind my head, "that we were hanging out with a few people from the paper," as she sat in my armchair with her legs crossed, "and watching the election results at Galapagos," slowly kicking her right leg back and forth, "and that I was going to sleep on your couch," with a blissful smile on her face. I frowned, "But I don't own a couch." She began rummaging through her purse, "I wanted to give you this," and pulled out a manuscript, "the guy she was with on Friday night wanted me to give you this story." I took a careful sip of coffee before asking, "He was with you last night as well?" "Yuck," she looked at me with disgust, "I've been carrying it around since then, and I was going to throw it away, but I think you should read it." My headache was coming back, "I'm not looking at any unsolicited work right now." "I don't want you to publish it..." She was adamant, "just read it." I stood up, "okay," slowly crossed the room, "okay," and took it out of her hand, "Jesus Christ." "I guess you're responsible in some way for what happened last night." I dropped the story on the pile of unsolicited fiction behind a row of bird guides, "How so?" Oscar entered the room and walked toward her shoes. "If you hadn't asked me to direct the play this would have never have happened." He smelled her outstretched hand before allowing her to caress him. "I really wish you wouldn't say that Cindy." She looked up from the cat, "Why not?" Steam rose from the Styrofoam cup. "Because you are very good at what you do," I sat down, "And what about the guy she was with on Friday night?" She shook her head, "That can't be serious." "Oh, but it is with you..." I clutched my forehead, "And why do you want to spend your time with someone that vapid?" Oscar jumped onto her lap. "Because she isn't really like the way we depicted her onstage... she isn't just one of your characters." Another plane flew above the windows. I closed my eyes, "she locked you out of her house Cindy," as the pale lights began to throb behind them, "and she lied to you." The co-pilot instructed the passengers to fasten their seatbelts as the plane descended through the patchy clouds. "I don't want to dwell on the past." The view from the cockpit revealed a low lying grid-work of houses, factory chimneys and incinerators that were spewing pale smoke. "Are you in love with her?" Slow moving traffic filled bridges spanning the East River and the broad expressways. "Maybe I am." The plane flew above the elevated subway lines as trains moved between the stations. "Well," I opened my eyes, " I really hope that she doesn't hurt you again." A runway bordered by blinking red lights approached rapidly in the diminishing distance.

First Friday in September

S tephanie was wearing a knee-length black dress and black pumps. A pink cashmere cardigan was neatly folded in the oversized black canvas purse by her feet. Alan saw her standing by the railing and facing the harbor. She was silhouetted by the silver glare of the sun reflecting off the water. He made his way through a group of tourists milling around the war memorial. Alan had called her at work on Tuesday morning, was told that she had taken a personal day, and left a message on her voicemail. She returned his call on Wednesday, after her boss had left for the day. She was unresponsive when he asked her out, yet he persisted, and she finally agreed to meet him after work on Friday in Bowling Green Park. Stephanie turned around when Alan said her name. She gave him her right hand, "How are you?" His reflection was cast in her circular sunglasses. He noted her thin smile, "I'm fine," and when he kissed her, "you're being so formal," she offered him her cheek. Stephanie turned toward the harbor, "I like coming here after work." A police helicopter flew past them. "Why is that?" She waited for the noise to fade, "it makes me feel grounded after being in the office all day." He regretted leaving his sunglasses in the glove compartment, "How is that working out?" Gulls hung on the breeze and wheeled overhead. "It's fine," she nodded, "I can't thank you enough for doing that for me." Sirens were caught up in the distant noise of traffic. "Well let's celebrate," he sank his hands into the front pockets of his khakis, "I've made dinner reservations for us at—" "—I haven't had much of an appetite lately," She pursed her lips. "What's wrong?" Alan thought of the call he made on Tuesday, "Are you trying to lose weight?" A ship's wake washed against the wall beneath them. "I can see your building from my office." "What floor are you on?" She turned around, "the ninety-second floor," and leaned against the railing, "I didn't realize that I was so afraid of heights until I started working there." The twin towers dominated the lower Manhattan skyline. "Isn't the view from up there a lot better than the panorama at the Queens Museum?" "Yeah I guess so," Stephanie nodded, "but my desk doesn't face the windows anymore," then quietly added, "and I haven't been out to the museum since we were there in June." A group of elderly women strolled past conversing in Polish. He shifted his feet, "that seems like a long time ago." Their shadows stretched across the shimmering asphalt. She brushed a lock of hair away from her mouth, "I guess it was," and tucked it behind her ear. "Not really," Alan clenched his jaw, "it was only three months." A group of teenage boys on roller blades wove between the groups of tourists. "You weren't afraid of heights when we had dinner at Windows on the World." A few pigeons were pecking apart a hot dog bun. "That was a different time," she shook her head dismissively, "But why are you saying this?" He turned to her, "because I really miss you." Raising her eyebrows, "now I'm confused." Alan removed his hands from his pockets, "we had a lot of fun together," and placed them on his waist. "You haven't even…" Stephanie removed her sunglasses, "when we last saw each other you made it clear that it was over," and fingered the tortoise shell frames, "and now we're going out to dinner to celebrate?" "Sure," he shrugged, "why not?" "What could we possibly be celebrating Alan," her heart was pounding in her throat "you were only interested in me when I was a convenient distraction," as she looked at him, "So what are we celebrating… Did you just buy a new car to drive me around in?" "Elaine and Olivia are out of town," he glanced at his watch, "and our dinner reservations are for seven-thirty." She thought of all the time she'd spent by the phone waiting for him to call, "So what?" It was six forty-five. "And I really miss having sex with you." She had wasted the summer on him, "you're a pig." He looked closely at her eyes and smiled, "That shouldn't be news to you." "You know that," she folded her arms across her stomach, "did you know that I had an abortion on Tuesday… That's why I wasn't at work when you called." He didn't blink, "Was it mine?" Shaking her head in disbelief, "what a stupid fucking question." He took a step back before asking, "Why did you agree to see me then?" "You know why Alan," she reached down and grabbed her purse, "because I really don't care about you anymore," then slung it over her shoulder, "and I *really* wanted you to know that."

The New Dress

J anet held the phone in her left hand, "I thanked him for the time we shared," while saying that she didn't think they were right for each other, "he sounded surprised at first," that she was very sorry, "and I don't think we talked for more than five minutes," but she really didn't want to see him anymore, "he took it well I guess," because it didn't feel like they were right for each other, "at least until the surprise wore off," suggesting that it probably had something to do with their difference in age, "but isn't it always that way," then assured James that he would be much happier with someone younger, "and then he asked if my decision had anything to do with you and I changed the subject," who was equally ambitious, "that was when he got angry with me," or a woman who could appreciate him for his writing, "and said that I was superficial," because to be perfectly honest there had been many times when his single-mindedness had really put her off, "he even called me vapid," and she countered by stating that she had never pretended to be an intellectual, "and claimed that I hadn't given him a chance," or had the slightest desire to continue being a cheerleader for an aspiring writer, "before hanging up on me."

Janet and James stood next to each other in front of the broad mirror in her lobby while she buttoned up her mink-lined wool coat and he ran a hand through his hair. Janet placed the phone on the side table and walked to the kitchen to mix herself a drink. He opened the black umbrella as the heavy front door banged behind them and then they stepped off her stoop in unison. "Oh my god," Cindy rolled her eyes, "he sounds like such a parasite," while recalling the clammy handshake that accompanied his hostile sneer, "but I guess I should be grateful for that," his dismissive opinion of the play, "because if he wasn't then you would have never been there," and how she had watched in dismay as Janet was dragged away before the second act began. She clutched his left arm and rested her head on his shoulder as they walked through the fog blanketing the neighborhood. Janet frowned before saying, "you mustn't gloat Cindy," like a teacher reprimanding her favorite pupil, "that's beneath you." James ticked the week's headlines off on the fingers of his free hand—Ashcroft's resignation, Arafat's death, the continuing assault in Falluja—while they waited on the corner for a series of cabs to pass through the intersection.

Janet filled the tall green glass with a few ice cubes, an ample amount of Gilbey's, a splash of tonic and a thin wedge of lime. Water droplets from a bare tree branch drummed on the umbrella that James held above their heads. Cindy really wanted to know what Janet had seen in him, "I'm not gloating." Janet asked if he was worried about being drafted. "You're not..." she offered Cindy the drink, "...Not even a little?" They crossed the cobblestone street as he claimed that it might be a good time to start befriending Canadians. Her bare feet left damp prints on the linoleum floor, "and then I took a shower," as she stood before Cindy in the spotless brightly lit kitchen, "as you can see," while drying her hair with a pink towel. Janet encouraged his interest in a potential move to Canada by telling him that if he lived there he wouldn't have to worry about not having health insurance. "Is that a new dress?" She then added that parts of Canada were quite beautiful. "Yes it is... I spoiled myself today... Do you like it?" The yellow flame from a gas lamp cast its wavering glow on the blue slate before and after their passing shadows. Cindy held up the plastic hanger, "You look great," the thin black velvet straps were clasped to, "especially without your makeup," and admired the simplicity of its design. The rich scent of crushed violets mingled with the lock of her hair that brushed the tip of his nose. Janet said, "you're the only person I know who says that."

He asked if she was interested in hearing about the story he had just begun. While fingering the price tag Cindy asked, "Are you going to wear it tonight?" She hoped that the evening wouldn't be dominated by another endless conversation about his writing while assuring him that he shouldn't have to ask. "It's such a cold night though," Janet placed a green bowl on the marble counter, "and it might be a bit formal," before cutting up the rest of the lime, "but I guess it depends on what you want to do." Another couple walked by them as he apologized for sounding so formal. "We can go get dinner and come back here," she crossed to the bedroom, "or find someplace in the neighborhood that's suitable for our quiet celebration." He told her how important her affection was to him and that the love they shared was extremely empowering. Cindy stood in the doorway and suggested, "or we could just have something delivered," as Janet removed the beige terry-cloth robe and placed it on the edge of the bed, "because I'm really not that hungry."

James claimed that the story he had just begun was loosely based on their relationship, it contained some of his best writing to date, and he had to thank her for that. She sprayed perfume, "I've been cooped up in here all day," on her throat and wrists, "so it would be nice to get some fresh air." Janet asked him just how close to their *relationship* this story actually was. She pulled open a drawer, "besides I'm starving," removed a black lace bra and a pair of matching panties, "and the fridge is practically empty." James assured her that he had no intention of exploiting her—that was the furthest thing from his mind. She looked at Cindy's reflection in the circular mirror hanging on the wall, "There's that new Brazilian place on Tenth Avenue," as she stepped into her panties, "Or we could go to Matsuri?"

Second Tuesday in September

The front door slammed behind Stephanie as she stepped off the brick steps. It was a warm cloudless morning. She walked to the 74th street station in a knee-length black cotton skirt and a light blue blouse. Her oversized black canvas purse was slung over her left shoulder and contained her pink cashmere cardigan, leather wallet, house keys, and a tuna fish sandwich that was packed in a pink Tupperware container. It was five after seven and a few people had already gathered outside the newsstand to buy lottery tickets. Campaign posters for the primary election had been stapled to the poles of the parking signs — both Fernando Ferrer and Mark Green wanted her vote that day. The black and white cat in the drugstore window watched her pass. An elderly woman scrubbed the sidewalk before the diner with a bucket of sudsy brown water and a push broom. A few workers outside the Korean market were filling the bins with peaches, plums, tomatoes and ears of corn. Muslim men with prayer mats rolled up beneath their arms were waiting for the bus. The advertisement on the side of the bus stop for a new antidepressant featured an attractive brunette in her early thirties standing in the center of an elegantly furnished living room, dressed in a beige business suit and speaking on a cordless phone. Four delivery trucks were idling outside the grocery store. A rat was lying motionless on the sidewalk with its eyes open.

The warmth of the sun on her shoulders and the glare flashing off the hoods and windows of the passing cars reminded her of meeting Alan for the first time. She waited near the curb for a livery cab to drive through the intersection and recalled their meeting in front of that shoe store in Soho last June. The pale salesgirl with the blue-black bob and almost British accent who rang up Stephanie's shoes complemented her purchase by claiming that she owned the exact same pair except in silver. Stephanie slipped her Visa into her wallet while the salesgirl slid the shoebox into a clear plastic bag. She crossed the showroom while eyeing the patent leather pumps on display, then pulled open the door and passed from the near-artic air conditioning into a humid afternoon on Mercer Street. The man she had noticed just outside the window stepped forward. "Hello there," he removed his hands from the front pockets of his black jeans, "I wouldn't normally do this," then glanced at the watch on his wrist, "but you look very familiar," as if he had been expecting her, "we've met before," then studied her eyes for a reassuring sign, "Haven't we?" She shook her head, "no, we haven't," and quickly walked around him.

Stephanie crossed against the light and continued walking toward the 74th street station. A sanitation inspector stood before an irate butcher in a bloodstained smock and endured a torrent of insults while writing up a summons. A large black garbage bag had been torn open and pieces of rotten meat and blackened vegetables were strewn along the sidewalk. She didn't want to get angry when she thought about Alan because that meant she still cared about him; what she really wanted was for the memories of their time together to vanish. What would her summer have been like if she *had* ignored him? She would still be temping in a downtown or mid-town office, worrying about how long the job was going to last and what work would come her way next. Her rent was due to go up a hundred dollars when her lease expired at the end of October. If she had simply walked by Alan that day, she wouldn't have gotten an abortion.

"Hello there," Alan removed his hands from the front pockets of his black jeans, "I wouldn't normally do this," then glanced at the watch on his wrist, "but you look very familiar," as if he had been expecting her, "we've met before," then studied her eyes for a reassuring sign, "Haven't we?" She *hated* being accosted on the street and quickly walked around him.

Stephanie waited for the signal to change as a slow moving street-sweeper gathered garbage from the gutter along Roosevelt Avenue and a Chevy Nova raced by in the opposite direction.

Alan sank his hands into the front pockets of his black jeans, "Hey Stephanie," and took a tentative step forward, "I'm really sorry about the way things turned out between us," before looking at her eyes, "I had no intention of hurting you and now I feel terrible about it… Can you ever forgive me for that?" "As if…" shaking her head in disbelief, "Don't you think it's a little late for that?" "Couldn't we just turn the corner here," the sleeves of his light green designer shirt were rolled up and exposed his muscular forearms, "Or maybe you just need some more time?" "That isn't very likely," Stephanie gave him a charitable, "and all you're doing right now is trying to make yourself feel better," yet dismissive smile, "and I'm afraid that isn't going to work on me again." "Well," Alan looked fleetingly at her legs, "I really miss all of the good times we had," and then eyed her mouth, "Don't you?" "You were drunk every time we were together," she surmised, "and I'm surprised that you remember anything at all." "I was just trying to have a good time," he stepped back, "Isn't that what you were doing?"

The woman who sold tamales from a shopping cart waited beside Stephanie and when the light changed they crossed the avenue beneath the elevated tracks. Stephanie removed the MetroCard from her purse and swiped it at the turnstile. She descended a flight of recently reconstructed stairs. Stepping onto the platform and walking through the crowds gathered by the stairs as a Manhattan bound E train pulled into the station. She continued along the platform as the train came to a slow screeching stop. A group of teenagers ambled out of the car before she could enter it along with two bleary-eyed Indian men in threadbare suits. She found a narrow place to stand and enough of the overhead bar to hold onto as the doors closed. A Chinese girl seated beneath her was sandwiched between two heavy-set black men. The girl's black hair was pulled back into pigtails and she was wearing a pink T-shirt with a grinning panda on the front, pink shorts with a smaller version of the same panda and a pair of scuffed pink sneakers that almost touched the floor. The smell of coffee filled the humid car while the surrounding bodies pressed into Stephanie and the train pulled away from the platform. The girl was engrossed in a copy of *Goodnight Dora* with illustrated cardboard flaps that pulled back to reveal sleepy woodland animals wishing Dora and her monkey sidekick Boots, "Goodnight," and "Buenas Noches" on the facing pages. The girl's older sister was seated nearby and listening to Madonna on a pair of headphones that were held together with Snoopy band-aids. Stephanie squeezed the bar with both hands while swaying to the train's rhythm as Dora and Boots continued their walk through the darkening woods. At 42nd Street Stephanie sat between a man who reeked of cigarettes and a young woman engrossed in a romance novel. Glancing over her shoulder *Claire closed her eyes and considered Grant's sinister proposition. She felt his eyes on her body as his twisted logic began to burn through her like a dozen blazing suns.* The man standing in front of Stephanie was working on the *Times* crossword. He was dressed in a dark blue oxford shirt, pleated khakis and polished loafers. The woman standing beside him was dressed in a new pair of Reeboks, pink tennis socks, a knee length beige skirt and a white silk blouse. A woman standing by the doors had a greenish butterfly tattoo on her right ankle. *Claire rolled onto her stomach and slowly undid her string bikini top. She knew that her bronzed body would distract him from his elaborate scheming. "Grant," Claire sighed, "be a dear and coat my back. It feels as if I'm melting."* The advertisement for the New York Language Center in Jackson Heights, a block away from the station where Stephanie boarded the train, featured a large color photograph of the earth. *A cool dollop of creamy coco-butter was smeared onto her shoulders. Grant's muscular hands moved slowly to her lower back where they lingered. "I think it's foolproof," Grant placed his hands on her narrow hips, "we'll cut him out of the picture by making him take the fall."* Feedback droned on the speakers for a long minute after the conductor announced the next station. *Grant's husky voice had a powerful hypnotic effect on Claire, "the take will be much larger without him,"* especially when his hands were massaging her well-toned flesh. Stephanie recalled sitting on a crowded East Hampton beach with Alan and being lectured on what she should study, when and if, she ever decided to go back to college. *Claire found herself nodding in agreement, "three is a crowd."* She thought about her husband and said, *"I always knew that he was expendable."*

Stephanie sat up on her beach towel and watched a set of waves roll against the shore. The sun was on her shoulders and suddenly all of Alan's self-aggrandizing advice was lost in the sounds of children shouting in the surf. A single engine plane pulled a wide Coppertone banner high above the shoreline. Stephanie watched the plane and its wavering banner gradually disappear in the blue distance. She looked over at Alan and discovered that he was gone. The surrounding scene had remained the same; another wave rolled against the shore, the family gathered beneath the large red and white umbrella continued eating their sandwiches and chips, and a few more seagulls had landed nearby to gobble up any scraps that might be thrown their way. The horizon still divided the sky and the sea but she no longer felt Alan's presence.

The woman with the romance novel got off at Canal Street and the seats on either side of her remained empty after the doors closed. She leaned back and clutched her purse in her lap as the train gradually picked up speed. Stephanie ignored the barefoot man panhandling for change, even though he was one of the regulars she sometimes gave money to, and closed her eyes. She was sitting cross-legged on a blue beach towel and watching a group of sandpipers pursuing a receding wave. The lightness in her chest that had replaced Alan caused her to smile. Sunlight glistened on a broad expanse of the sea as a few cumulus clouds hung motionless above the horizon. Stephanie opened her eyes as the train came to a slow screeching stop and yawned into her left hand before standing up. The conductor announced that it was exactly eight o'clock and reminded the passengers to take all of their personal belongings with them as they filed out of the car. The doors closed as she walked along the platform. A Queens-bound E train on the opposite track slowly pulled out of the station as she climbed a flight of stairs. She rode an escalator up to the bank of express elevators and one of them carried her to the ninety-second floor.

Acknowledgments

With gratitude to Johannah Rodgers, Susan Daitch, Barney Rosset, Astrid Myers, Mónica de la Torre, Betsy Sussler, Yasmine Alwan, Eugene Lim, Theodore Hamm, Phong Bui, Bruce Pearson, Ted Pelton, Rebecca Maslen and Ed Taylor.

"Mid-April and late October" appeared in *Tantalum*; "An Older Lover—Act 1" appeared in *Harp and Altar,* "Labor Day and Cold Spring" and "Exclusion Apply—Part 3" (under the working title of "The Last Memory of My Father") appeared in *The Evergreen Review*; "First Friday in June", "Fourth Thursday in July", "First Friday in September" and "Second Tuesday in September" appeared in *BOMB*.

Recent Starcherone titles:

The Twilight of the Bums by George Chambers
& Raymond Federman
A Heaven of Others by Joshua Cohen
PP/FF by Peter Conners, ed.
Dear Ra by Johannes Göransson
The Blue of Her Body by Sara Greenslit
Quinnehtukqut by Joshua Harmon
The Lost Books of the Odyssey by Zachary Mason

purchase through
www.starcherone.com
www.spdbooks.org
www.amazon.com
or
P.O. Box 303
Buffalo, NY 14201-0303

Starcherone Books is a signatory to the Book Industry
Treatise on Responsible Paper Use, the goal of which
is to increase use of postconsumer recycled fiber from
a 5% average at present to a 30% average by 2011.

Starcherone Books is a non-profit whose mission
is to promote innovative fiction writers and encourage
the growth of their audiences. Information about the
press and our authors, ordering books, contributing to
our non-profit, and other initiatives in furtherance of
our public-spirited mission may be seen at
www.starcherone.com.

Starcherone Books
PO Box 303
Buffalo, NY 14201